Nate was ⸻⸻⸻ in. He
stopped ar⸻⸻⸻ds for
what he was seeing ⸻ covered
much of the ground, inches of it, to within five or
six yards of their front door. At first it appeared as
if the water was moving, but it wasn't the water; it
was something *in* the water. He took a few steps
and the shapes acquired form. "It can't be," he
blurted.

"You see them, then?"

Nate nodded. Snakes. Rattlesnakes. Hundreds
of the things, swimming, crawling, moving aimlessly about as if they had no sense of where they
should go. "God in heaven."

The Wilderness series:

WILDERNESS #63:
VENOM

David Thompson

LEISURE BOOKS NEW YORK CITY

Dedicated to Judy, Joshua and Shane.
And to Beatrice Bean, with the most loving regard.

A LEISURE BOOK®

March 2010

Published by

Dorchester Publishing Co., Inc.
200 Madison Avenue
New York, NY 10016

ISBN 10: 0-8439-6263-1
ISBN 13: 978-0-8439-6263-5
E-ISBN: 978-1-4285-0824-8

The name "Leisure Books" and the stylized "L" with design are trademarks of Dorchester Publishing Co., Inc.

Printed in the United States of America.

10 9 8 7 6 5 4 3 2

Visit us online at www.dorchesterpub.com.

WILDERNESS #63:
VENOM

Prologue

She was sleek and gorgeous and five feet long.

It was late summer in the Rocky Mountains. The sun blazed in a cloudless sky.

The female lay curled on a flat rock in a gully. The temperature hovered near one hundred degrees. Where most creatures would swelter, she thrived; she soaked up the heat as a sponge soaked up water.

A hawk screeched, causing the female to crawl under a nearby boulder. She didn't have ears, but she was conscious of the vibrations the hawk's cry created in the air. They were absorbed through her skin, muscle and bone to her inner ear. For a while she stayed in the relative coolness under the boulder, but she didn't like the cool as much as the heat and she crawled back out to her rock and curled her body.

The female darted her forked tongue in and out and discovered she was no longer alone. Her tongue picked up scents and carried them to a tiny organ in the back of her mouth and the organ told her what the scent was.

A male, and it was close.

The female raised her head and looked about. Her eyesight wasn't exceptional. She could see about ten times her body length. Beyond that was murky. But her kind didn't rely solely on hearing and sight. She had another sense. Between her eyes and her false nostrils were pits that detected the body heat given off by other creatures. Her pits confirmed what her tongue and her eyes had told her.

Long and thick, the male twined down the side of the gully. His tongue kept flicking. He knew she was there, and he was coming for her. He had caught the special scent she gave off.

The female stayed coiled. He was almost to her when another male appeared. The second male had sensed her, too, and was intent on the same purpose. Both males stopped and swung their heads toward each other. The first male raised his head high. The second did the same. They slithered close and stopped.

The female watched. She had no part in what was to come. She did not get to pick.

Edging forward, the two males raised half their bodies off the ground, as if each was seeking to show that it was taller than its rival. They hissed and flicked their tongues and slowly pressed against each other. Swaying like reeds in a wind, they entwined. The first male tried to push the second male to the ground. The second male slipped free and sought to do the same to the first male.

Neither would relent until it had pinned its rival.

The female had witnessed the ritual many times. When the males were the same size it could go on a long time. She could be patient. She would wait as long as it took.

Eventually the first male won. He was bigger and the bigger males always won, but the smaller males never stopped trying.

The female lay still as the male joined her on the rock. He nudged her with his head, and when she didn't bare her fangs he crawled up and over and on top of her. He nudged her a few times. After a while she uncoiled.

The male ran his body along hers and she ran hers along his. When she was ready she lay still and the male slid into position.

The female felt little. To her it was not pleasure but a necessity. She must do it to have young and to give birth to young was one of the foremost drives of her life. When the male was done he lay next to her for a space. Then, with a parting flick and a hiss, he was gone.

The female stayed where she was. She lay soaking up the sun until it was so low in the sky that the gully was plunged in twilight. The heat began to dissipate. She crawled off her rock and around the boulder and down the side of the gully to a cleft. It was not much wider than she was. She crawled into it and along a winding course that brought her to a large underground chamber.

Others of her kind were there. It was their haven, their breeding area, their den. It was where the females gave birth. All of her kind for many leagues around came to the den to winter over. Some winters there were more than others. This past winter there had been the most ever. Many had since dispersed and would gather again when the weather turned cold. Many more remained to roam the gully and the surrounding area. They formed an enormous roiling mass, entwining with one another, each as deadly as any creature could be.

For most of the summer they had lived as they always did, and all was well. Then the intruders came.

Chapter One

"Land sakes, it's pretty," Emala Worth declared. She sat astride a mare on a ridge overlooking a valley as beautiful as anything. Miles-high peaks, some crowned by ivory mantles of snow, bastioned the valley from the outside world. Thick woods covered the lower slopes and green grass covered the valley floor. The topaz blue of a pristine lake gleamed bright in the sunlight. "Isn't it, Samuel?"

Samuel Worth grunted. They had taken forever to cross the prairie and come deep into the mountains, and now that they had finally arrived, he didn't see much difference between the valley and the savage wilderness they had spent weeks penetrating.

"Nothin' to say?" Emala goaded. "You're the one wanted this. You're the one had his heart set on livin' free."

"Don't start," Samuel warned. A big man, he wore a homespun shirt she had made and pants bought with money given him by his new friend Nate King. Samuel shifted in his saddle and said to his benefactor, "So you say this valley is named after you?"

"King Valley," Nate confirmed. He was as big as Samuel but broader at the shoulders. His attire consisted of buckskins and moccasins and an eagle feather tied in his hair. A powder horn, ammo pouch and possibles bag crisscrossed his chest. In the crook of his elbow rested a Hawken rifle and around his waist was a virtual armory: two flintlock pistols, a Bowie knife and a tomahawk. "Shakespeare, here, started calling it that, and the handle stuck."

The man Nate referred to was a fellow mountain man, Nate's mentor and best friend in all creation, Shakespeare McNair. McNair was similarly attired and armed but had white hair to Nate's black. "That I did, hoss. I could just as well have called it Nate's Slice of Heaven." He chuckled and quoted his namesake. "What's in a name? That which we call a rose by any other name would smell as sweet."

"I can't get over how funny you talk," Emala said. "Half the time I can't understand you."

Nate laughed. "Don't feel bad. No one else can understand him either."

Shakespeare harrumphed and resorted to the Bard again. "Scoff on, vile fiend and shameless courtesan."

"Now see," Emala said. "Who talks like that?"

"You have to forgive him," Nate said. "He's getting on in years and sometimes the aged become touched in the head."

"*Aged?*" Shakespeare squawked, and looked fit to burst a blood vessel. "I will bite thee by the ear for that jest."

Samuel had noticed brown structures along the lakeshore. "Which cabins do you all live in?"

Nate answered him. "I live on the west side of the lake, my son and his wife on the north shore. The cabin to the south is Shakespeare's. Waku and his family live to the east."

Samuel glanced behind him at the family in question, five Nansusequa Indians who had fled across the Mississippi River when the rest of their tribe was wiped out and their village destroyed by whites who wanted their land. They had been living in King Valley for some time now.

Chickory Worth, Samuel's son, kneed his mount forward. "Where will we have our cabin, Mr. King?"

Nate studied the boy. Chickory had recently come down sick with a high fever and the chills. For ten days the fourteen-year-old hovered near death at Bent's Fort. Nate had been returning alone from a trip to the geyser country and been surprised to find McNair and his daughter and the Worths and the Nansuseqas all there, waiting for Chickory to recover. Like the rest, he had been stumped by the boy's illness. No one could say what brought it on. "Wherever your ma and pa would like," he said. "How are you feeling, by the way?"

"Fine as can be," Chickory said.

Two other members of their party—Nate's daughter, Evelyn, and Chickory's older sister, Randa—brought their horses up next to Nate's.

"Why have we stopped, Pa?" Evelyn asked. "I can't wait to get home. After what we've been through, I don't know as how I'll ever leave here again."

Nate smothered a grin. This was the same girl who once wanted to forsake the mountains and live in a city. "Lead the way," he said. He couldn't wait to get home either. He dearly missed his wife.

The trail wound through ranks of tall fir and shadowed spruce and pine. Squirrels scampered in the high branches. Jays squawked raucously. Finches warbled and sparrows chirped. Twice startled deer bounded away with their tails up and once a cow elk and her well-grown calf went crashing off through the brush.

Nate breathed deep of the clear mountain air.

This was his home, his haven, as near to paradise on earth as he'd ever found. He loved it here and intended to stay the rest of his days.

In half an hour they emerged from the forest near the Nansusequa lodge.

Nate bid his friends good-bye and continued along the south shore to Shakespeare's cabin. McNair invited the Worths in, and they agreed. As Emala put it, "I can dearly use some rest from all this ridin'. My backside wasn't made for sittin' a horse."

That left Nate and Evelyn free to make the short ride to their own cabin, where he wearily drew rein.

Inside, Winona King was baking when she heard them ride up. She took off the apron her husband had bought her in St. Louis and hurried out.

Nate swung down and turned just as the cabin door opened. Warmth flooded his chest, as if his heart were on fire. He drank in the sight of her shimmering ink-black hair and the beaded buckskin dress that accented the beauty of the body it clothed, a body he knew as well as he knew his own. "Winona," he said softly, and spread his big arms.

Winona melted into them and hugged him close. "Husband," she said simply.

Nate sniffed her hair, savoring the scent. He felt whole again.

"I have missed you," Winona said.

"And I you."

"Was there any trouble?"

"No more than usual," Nate hedged. Later he would tell her about the scalp hunters who nearly slew their daughter and the hostiles who had tried to take his own life.

Evelyn climbed down and let her reins dangle. "You two can stand there forever, but I want a bath and a hot meal and good night's sleep." She started toward the door.

"Where do you think you're going, young lady?" Winona asked.

"You know the rules," Nate said. "Your animal comes first. Strip your saddle and put him in the corral and then we'll fill the basin."

"Aw, Pa." Evelyn had hankered for a bath for days now.

"You heard your father," Winona said.

Evelyn snatched the reins and led her horse around to the corral. She was mildly annoyed. Here she was, sixteen years old, and her parents treated her as if she were ten. She thought about her recent trip to the prairie with the Nansusequas, and felt herself blush. Thank goodness her folks didn't know about Dega and her. She imagined they would be upset, her kissing a boy.

Evelyn closed her eyes, remembering. Oh, those kisses. She never experienced anything like them. They had left her breathless, they were so potent. She couldn't get enough.

Evelyn opened her eyes and giggled. She was in love, in honest-to-God love. She'd never expected anything like this to happen to her. Oh, sure, women fell in love all the time. But somehow she'd always thought she would be different. Grinning at the memory of those wonderful kisses, she leaned her rifle against a post, opened the gate, and ushered her horse into the corral. She undid the cinch and took off the saddle and threw it over the top rail. She did the same with the saddle blanket, then removed the bridle. She patted the horse and went out and closed the gate. She turned to reclaim her rifle, and froze.

A rattlesnake was almost at her feet.

* * *

"Younguns," Nate said as his daughter led her horse around the corner. "You would think she'd know better by now."

"Blue Flower is not a child anymore, husband," Winona said in her impeccable English, using their daughter's Shoshone name. "She is almost a woman."

"The 'almost' is the important part," Nate said. "I'd as soon she stayed as she is for five or six years yet."

"We have both seen how she looks at Dega. It would not surprise me if she agrees to be his wife."

Nate was genuinely shocked. "She's not old enough for that. Not by a long shot."

"Girls in some tribes marry even younger," Winona reminded him. "So do many whites."

"I don't much care what everyone else does," Nate grumbled. He never had patterned his behavior by how others acted.

Winona put her hand on his shoulder and looked him in the eyes. "I understand this upsets you. It would upset me, too, were it not, as you whites would say, the natural order of things."

"I should have a talk with Dega. Find out what his intentions are."

"You will do no such thing," Winona cautioned. "It would embarrass her. Did my father ask you your intentions before we went out at night to stand under a blanket?"

Nate grinned at the recollection. "I've never been so fond of a blanket in my life."

"You are avoiding the issue."

"What's embarrassing," Nate said, "is that you speak my tongue better than I do. I hardly ever use the word 'issue.' Or 'avoid,' for that matter."

"You do not fool me, Nathaniel King."

"Whenever you get formal I know I'm in trouble."

Winona kissed him on his chin. "You may not use those words, but you know them. You are a reader. We have more books in our cabin than anyone in the Rockies."

"Twenty-seven isn't a lot."

"Shakespeare has only one."

"Yes, and he's been reading it for thirty years. No wonder he has the darn thing memorized."

Winona laughed and kissed him again, on the cheek. "Have I told you today how much I love you?"

"I have two cheeks."

Winona kissed him on the other. "But you are still avoiding the issue. You think that by talking about something else I will not notice, but I do."

"You're female."

"What does that mean?"

"Women notice everything. It's why men get in so much trouble."

"Men get in trouble because they are men." Winona kissed him full on his lips. "Now back to Evelyn. We both know how she feels about Dega. We see it in her eyes when she looks at him and hear it in her voice when she talks about him."

"Could be it won't last," Nate said hopefully. "Could be I'll be an old man before she thinks about taking a husband."

Winona tilted her head skyward and pointed. "Look there!" she cried.

All Nate saw was blue, save for a puffy pillow of a cloud off in the distance. "What did you see?"

"A flying cow."

Nate couldn't help himself. He cackled, then forced

a sober expression and said, "I take it that was your notion of a hint."

"Was I too subtle?"

"My God, the words you use. Have you been reading my books when I'm not around?"

"*Ne tsaawesunga baide suwai Degamawaku,*" Winona said in Shoshone.

Nate struggled to recollect what *tsaawesunga* meant. "You do? You really feel good about Evelyn and Dega being together?"

"He is a good boy. Good in heart and good in mind. She has chosen as I chose you."

"Wait, wait, wait," Nate said. "After all these years you're telling me you became my wife because you thought I have a good heart?"

"I do not think you do. I know you do. You have the best heart of all the men I have ever met, red or white."

"Shakespeare has a good heart."

"It belongs to Blue Water Woman. And he is old enough to be my grandfather. I wanted a slightly younger man for my husband."

"*Slightly* younger? Why, you wench, you." Nate patted her posterior. "Let me put my horse in the corral and I'll show you who is old."

"In broad daylight? With our daughter in the cabin?"

Nate glanced up. "Where is she, anyhow? She should have been back by now."

"Maybe she is brushing her horse."

"Without being told?" Nate scoffed. He kissed Winona and tugged on the reins and made for the side of their cabin. "I'd better check on her."

"I will fix a meal. If she has gone off to see Dega, don't be mad. Young love does foolish things."

Nate walked faster. He was willing to admit that Winona had a point, but he still wasn't comfortable with the idea of his daughter being interested in a man, no matter how good the man's heart might be. She was his little girl. She would always be his little girl. He saw her standing at the corral gate, and smiled. "There you are. We were wondering where you got to."

Evelyn didn't respond or move.

"What the devil has gotten into . . ." Nate began, and felt a chill ripple down his spine when a blunt triangular head rose a few inches off the ground. He snapped his Hawken to his shoulder and thumbed back the hammer but didn't shoot. At that angle the slug might go through the snake and hit Evelyn in the leg. Slowly circling, he said quietly, "Don't move a muscle. I'll take care of our visitor."

"Don't kill it, Pa."

Nate stopped. "Why in blazes not? It's a rattler. One less won't be missed." He had seen two or three since summer began. One morning he nearly stepped on one on his way to the chicken coop to collect eggs; he had chopped off its head with his ax.

"It hasn't tried to bite me." Evelyn didn't like snakes all that much, but she didn't like to kill at all.

"It's a *rattler*," Nate said again.

"So? If it's not bothering us, why must you kill it? It has as much right to live as we do."

"Where do you get those strange notions of yours?" Nate took another step and had the shot he wanted.

"Please, Pa."

"What if it sticks around and bites my horse or your horse or your mother?" Nate was glad Winona hadn't heard him mention her last. He would be in for no end of barbed tongue.

"You don't know that it will. You just want an excuse to shoot it."

Nate lowered the Hawken. "That was harsh. I don't go around killing for the sake of killing things. I only do it when it's necessary."

"Is it truly necessary now?"

Nate scowled. She had him. The snake wasn't hissing or rattling or doing anything except stare at her. "All right. Shoo it off. But if you get bit, don't come crying to me."

Evelyn took hold of her rifle and bent and poked at the rattler. Instantly, it reared and its tail buzzed. She poked at it again and it retreated, whipping its body from side to side.

"Careful," Nate cautioned.

"Isn't he beautiful, Pa?"

Nate had never thought of snakes as anything but, well, *snakes*. This one was about three feet long with splashes of dark brown edged with black. Its vertical pupils lent its face a vicious cast, as if it couldn't wait to sink its fangs into something. He would just as soon shoot it and be done with it.

Evelyn jabbed and took another step—and the rattler did the last thing she expected. It launched itself under her rifle at her legs.

Chapter Two

Nate reacted purely on reflex. He drew a pistol and fired from the hip. He didn't think, he didn't aim, he pointed and shot and the rattlesnake's head exploded in a shower of gore.

Evelyn had started to recoil. Bits of snake spattered her arms and face and a piece of snake flesh flew into her mouth and partway down her throat. Gagging, she doubled over and nearly swallowed it.

All Nate could think of was how close she had come to being bitten. He put his hand on her shoulder and asked, "Are you all right?"

Evelyn couldn't talk. She was coughing and hacking, trying to dislodge the piece. Her stomach contracted and she nearly vomited. She tasted bitter bile, and coughed some more, and the grisly tidbit shot out of her mouth and into her hand. "Lord," she breathed, afraid she would be sick.

The headless body was thrashing about. In a fit of anger, Nate placed his boot on it and mashed it into the dirt. The body ruptured, spewing its insides. He kicked it away in disgust.

"Thanks, Pa," Evelyn said.

"I told you. Rattlers aren't to be trusted."

Winona came around the corner wearing her apron, her rifle in hand. "Why did you shoot?" she anxiously asked.

Nate nodded at the viper. "Our youngest nearly got herself bit."

Incredibly, the snake was still moving. Winona walked up to it and remarked, "Another rattlesnake? I saw a couple while you were away. And Blue Water Woman was saying how she's seen more this year than in any year she can remember."

"Maybe we should have a hunt," Nate suggested. If there were that many rattlers around, they needed to be thinned out. "Kill as many as we can so we don't have to worry about stepping on one in the dark."

Evelyn was beginning to feel a little better. She uncurled and ran her sleeve over her mouth. "Can't we leave them be? The only reason this one tried to bite me is because I was poking it."

"We'll talk later," Nate said. He caught Winona's eye and motioned. She immediately understood.

Gently taking Evelyn's arm, Winona said, "Come inside, Daughter. We will heat water for your bath, and I will cook venison and wild asparagus for our supper."

Nate stripped his bay and the packhorse and put them in the corral with the others. He had been in the saddle most of the day and could stand to stretch his legs. On a whim he walked to the lake. Out on the water ducks and geese paddled placidly about. A fish leaped clear and dived. An eagle glided down and rose up again, flapping strongly, a fish in its talons.

Nate strolled along the shore. It felt wonderful to be home. He'd missed the valley, missed the serenity. He didn't fool himself, though. In the shadowed ranks of the thick forest prowled bears and mountain lions and wolves. Hostiles could pay them a visit at any time. Then there was Nature herself, as temperamental a mistress as ever unleashed a tempest.

Peace in the wilderness was the exception, not the

norm, a condition to be savored as someone might savor a fine wine or brandy.

Nate was a master at savoring. The hardships he'd endured over the years had taught him the value of stopping to smell the roses now and then, a lesson some people never learned. They became so caught up in life that they forgot it was meant to be lived.

"Say there, mister. Don't I know you from somewhere?"

Nate was so deep in thought, he hadn't realized he was no longer alone. He looked up and smiled. "Zach!"

"Me," his son said. "I saw riders and figured it must be you. You were gone an awful long time." Not quite as tall or as broad as Nate, Zach was swarthy enough to pass for a full-blooded Indian. His eyes, though, betrayed his white half; they were a piercing green.

They hugged. Nate had never been averse to showing that he cared for his loved ones. Some men were. Some hardly ever hugged their wives and children, and thought the little they did was more than enough.

"I've missed you, Pa," Zach said warmly, clapping his father on the back. "I wish I could have gone with you."

"You know you couldn't. Not with your wife in the family way." Nate studied him. "What have you been up to while I was gone?"

"Not much. I had a scrape with the Indians in the next valley. And a Blood warrior stole Louisa, but I got her back. Other than that, things have been quiet."

"You don't say." Nate hid his alarm. Unlike Shakespeare, who exaggerated everything, Zach tended to make molehills out of mountains. "You and your missus are invited to our place tonight to tell us all about it."

"If Louisa is up to it," Zach said. "She has started to show, and some days she is sickly."

"Your mother had her bouts, too," Nate told him. "Carrying a baby wears women down." It would wear him down. The swelling, the sickness, the need to eat for two instead of one; he didn't know how women bore it.

"Listen to us." Zach chuckled. "Talking about making babies instead of lifting scalps."

"I thought you gave that up."

"I have," Zach said. "For now."

Nate decided to change the subject. "Tell me something. Have you seen many snakes around this summer?"

"What kind? I saw a few garters and a black snake and the tail end of what might have been a pine snake."

"The tail end?"

"It was going down a hole."

A raven flew over, the swish of its wings loud in the rarefied mountain air.

"How about rattlers?" Nate asked.

"Come to think of it, I've seen a few."

"How many, exactly?" Nate pressed him.

"What does it matter? We see rattlers a lot."

"It's important," Nate urged.

Zach scratched his chin. "Let's see. Nine or ten, I reckon, since the weather warmed."

"That's more than usual, isn't it?"

"I suppose. I don't pay much attention. You've seen one snake, you've seen them all. Why?"

"I'm thinking of organizing a rattlesnake hunt," Nate revealed.

Zach snorted in amusement. "Are you giving up buffalo and elk and deer for snake meat?"

"There are too many around."

"There are too many chipmunks, too. Do we exterminate them next?"

"Very funny. But your sister was almost bit."

"If she was, I'd feel sorry for the snake," Zach joked. "Likely as not, *she* would poison *it*."

"Now, now," Nate said.

"I don't see the sense to it, but if you want to hunt rattlers, count me in. Someone has to watch your back so one doesn't bite you in the behind."

Nate gazed to the north at his son's distant cabin. Wisps of smoke rose from the stone chimney. "How is Lou coming along otherwise?"

"Fine. She swears she can feel the baby kick, but it can't be nowhere near big enough yet."

"You'll make a fine father," Nate predicted.

"So she says and so Uncle Shakespeare says and so Ma says and so you say," Zach recited without much conviction.

"You don't sound as sure."

Zach looked out over the lake and then at the sky and then down at the tips of his moccasins. "Do you want the truth?" he quietly asked.

"Always."

"I'm scared, Pa. More than I've ever been scared. I have an awful feeling I won't make a good father at all."

Nate stood next to him, their shoulders nearly touching, and pretended to be interested in the lake. A male and female mallard were a short ways out, swimming side by side. "Why won't you?"

"I'm not ready. I have a temper, remember? I've done things that have gotten me in a lot of trouble."

"When we're young we all do things we wouldn't do when we are older. It's normal."

"Is it normal to be taken into custody by the army and put on trial for murder?"

"Well, no."

"Is it normal to have to make worm food of as many people as I have and get a reputation as a killer?"

"Hold on," Nate said. "When a hostile is out to count coup on you or a white man is out to slit your throat because he doesn't like that you are half-and-half, you have to defend yourself."

"I don't feel guilty over any of that. I'm just saying I might not be fit to be a good father. Not like you. For long as I can remember, whenever I needed you, there you were. Always ready to help. Just as you're trying to help me now."

"You're my son," Nate said.

"I don't know as I have it in me to do the same with mine."

"We never do until we're put to the test. I didn't know when I married your mother that I'd be a good father. Best I can recall, I was as scared as you. I thought I would mess up. I thought she was crazy to think I wouldn't. But she was right, as she nearly always is."

"Ma is smart, that's for sure."

"The secret is to take it one day at a time. Do the best you can each of those days and let the rest take care of themselves."

Zach frowned. "I'll try. But I wish I had your confidence."

"You do. You just don't know it yet." Nate put a hand on his son's shoulder. "Is that all that's bothering you?"

"It's enough. But no. There's more. There's the other big thing."

"I'm listening."

"The blood thing."

"Oh. That."

"All my life I have had to put up with people hating me because I'm a breed. Whites hate breeds because we're part Indian and a lot of Indians hate breeds because we're half white."

"There is a lot of stupid in this world," Nate said.

"There's more stupid than smart," Zach said. "Look at what it did to me. It got so I'd hanker to shoot anyone who so much as looked at me crosswise. I got to hate the haters as much as they hated me."

"You have remarkable restraint. There's a good chunk of the population still breathing who shouldn't be."

Zach chuckled. "Sometimes you sound like Uncle Shakespeare."

"That's scary."

"Seriously, Pa. I don't put up with people hating me and I am damn sure not going to put up with people hating my boy or girl because they happened to be born of mixed-blood parents."

"You're getting ahead of yourself. Look at you and your sister. You are half-and-half, and it shows. Your sister is half-and-half, and it doesn't. She took more after my side of the family. It could be your child will be like her. Or maybe your mother's side will come through and she will look to be a full-blooded Indian and no one will guess the truth."

"I doubt that. I'm only half and Lou is all white so maybe our kid will be as you say, like Evelyn."

"You have an issue with that?"

"An issue?"

"I'm trying to talk like your mother so everyone will think I'm as smart as she is."

"Oh. No, I meant an issue how? I don't resent the red part of me, if that's what you're saying. There are days when I liked it more than the white part."

"Those must be the days I made you clean your room."

"I just want my boy or girl to be happy. I want them to have a good life."

"See? You're doing it already."

"Doing what?"

"Being a good father and your baby hasn't even been born yet."

Zach smiled. "You have a knack. I hope I do half as good as you."

"Take each problem as it comes up and don't fret, and you'll do just fine," Nate predicted.

They were silent a bit, watching the waterfowl, until Zach said, "Care to come say hi to Lou? She'll be tickled to see you."

"I would like that, yes," Nate said.

As they turned, someone yelled Nate's name. Winona had come back out and was beckoning.

"Ma wants you." Zach stated the obvious.

"And when she cracks her whip, I flinch."

"Oh, Pa."

"Tell Lou I'll visit later."

Nate hurried over. He had lived with his wife for so long and knew her so well that he could tell when something was urgent. "Are we under attack?"

"Shakespeare needs you. He sent her to fetch you," Winona said, nodding toward Randa Worth.

Randa was about Evelyn's age, a sleek young girl about to bloom as a woman. It was her blooming that had gotten the Worths in trouble. One of the plantation owners had taken a fancy to her. Samuel slew the man to keep her from being raped and the family had to run for their lives.

"What's wrong?" Nate asked.

"It's one of his horses," Randa said. "It's dead and he wanted you to come see."

"What killed it? A mountain lion?"

"No, sir. He thinks maybe it was a rattlesnake."

Chapter Three

The mare lay on her side at the back of the corral. She had died sometime early the night before, and her body was stiff and starting to bloat and gave off a smell. She would smell a lot worse before another day was out. It wasn't the white mare McNair usually rode. It was a pack animal.

"What do you think?" Shakespeare asked.

Nate was examining a leg. "I think this is a horse."

Shakespeare snorted. "Wilt thou show the whole wealth of thy wit in an instant?" he quoted.

"At least you say it's wit."

"I was being charitable, Horatio." Shakespeare touched a spot on the mare's front leg below the knee. "Right there. Do those look like puncture marks to you?"

Nate bent close. "Could be. But if they are, it couldn't have been a big snake."

"Small rattlers are as deadly as the big ones," Shakespeare mentioned. "It's not their size. It's the venom."

His wife, Blue Water Woman, was coming toward them. Over by the cabin Winona was talking to Samuel and Emala Worth.

Blue Water Woman was a Flathead. She wore a buckskin dress fashioned different from Winona's; the waist was higher and it had longer sleeves, and where Winona liked blue beads, Blue Water Woman had decorated her dress with red and yellow. Her arms were folded across her bosom. "I am sorry, husband," she said to McNair.

"For what, pray tell?"

"I should have noticed sooner."

"How so? You told me the horses were fine when you checked on them last evening. And when you came out this morning the others were milling near the gate and blocked your view so you couldn't have seen her lying here."

"I should have been more observant," Blue Water Woman said. "I feel bad."

"Did you see any snakes near your cabin while we were away?" Nate asked. "Any rattlesnakes."

"Now that you mention it, yes. I saw two. A big one not long after Shakespeare and you left, over near the woods. And a small one just a few sleeps ago, by the woodpile."

"The woodpile, you say?"

Nate and Shakespeare looked at each other. They walked out of the corral and around McNair's cabin to a high stack of firewood, mostly pine and oak. The others followed.

An ax was leaning against the logs. At one end the stack had collapsed and dozens were in a heap.

"Odds are it's gone," Shakespeare said.

"Sometimes they find a spot they like and stick," Nate said. He nudged a log with his foot and stooped and rolled a few from the pile. "Maybe it's still in here." He reached for another log and a thin bolt of scales and fangs shot out from between two others. There was no warning. No rattling or hissing. He jerked his hand back but wasn't quick enough. The fangs sank into his sleeve.

"Nate!" Winona cried.

Emala Worth screamed.

Nate whipped his arm from side to side but the rattlesnake clung on. It had no choice; its fangs were caught fast.

"Horatio!" Shakespeare bellowed, and pointed at the ground.

Nate placed his arm flat. The viper twisted and squirmed and rattled, frantic to free itself.

"Let me," Shakespeare said, and stepped on it, pinning it behind the head. "Now you can pull it off."

Instead Nate drew his Bowie. He tapped the tip on McNair's moccasin and Shakespeare moved his foot half an inch. Nate slashed, severing the head from the body. Shakespeare raised his leg and the body went on twisting and whipping about.

"Oh Lordy!" Emala exclaimed.

Nate raised his arm and stared at the head. The head stared back. He sheathed the Bowie and reached over his wrist and tried to pry off the head. It was stuck fast.

Winona came to his side and placed her warm hand on his. "Are you all right?"

Nate nodded.

"It didn't bite you?"

"It tried real hard." Nate smiled and kissed her on the check and she surprised him considerably by kissing him on the mouth. She rarely did that around others.

"It scared me," Winona said.

"It scared me, too."

Shakespeare chortled and said, "But soft, what light through yonder window breaks! It is the east, and Juliet is the sun!"

"That was sweet of you," Winona said.

"Why is it he never quotes that to me?" Blue Water Woman asked.

"Uh-oh," Shakespeare said.

They all laughed.

Emala Worth stared at each of them and shook her head. "How can you be so happy after Mr. King was nearly bit? That was awful. I thought my heart would stop."

"Rattlesnake bites don't always kill," Nate remarked.

"They do often enough that most people don't keep them as pets," Shakespeare said.

"Most?" Winona repeated.

"I knew a Southern gent years ago. Before I ever came west. He kept a dozen or so in a shack. Used them in their church service."

Winona showed her confusion. "A church, you say? I have seen them when my husband took me to St. Louis. It is where whites worship the Great Mystery."

"I was raised Mennonite," Shakespeare said. "We had a meeting hall, but it was the same thing."

"Why do whites use snakes in a church? Nate has never told me that."

"He tends to be forgetful," Shakespeare said. "Infants often are."

Winona actually giggled.

"I am right here," Nate said.

"The snakes?" Winona said to McNair.

"You're familiar with the Bible? I know Horatio has a copy in his little library—"

"Little?" Nate said.

"I am familiar with it," Winona responded. "I

have not read it through as he has, but he has read much of it to me and I have read a little on my own. I speak the white tongue much better than I read or write it."

"You are a marvel," Shakespeare said. "But back to the Bible. In it are all sorts of sayings about what we should and shouldn't do. Thou shalt not bear false witness. Thou shalt not kill. Love thy neighbor as thyself. Be perfect as thy Father in heaven is perfect."

"Does it mention snakes?"

"There's the serpent in the Garden of Eden, the one who tricks Eve into taking a bite of the forbidden fruit. Some folks say that wasn't a serpent at all but Satan."

"Nate has told me about him. Satan is the one whites say brings much evil into the world."

"Has he told you about the part where people who believe in the Almighty can handle snakes?"

"I do not remember him ever saying anything about that, no."

"Tsk, tsk," Shakespeare said to Nate.

Winona turned. "I do not understand, husband. What kind of snakes does the Bible say they can pick up?"

"It's in one of the four Gospels," Nate explained. "Toward the end of Mark. It says that those who believe will be able to cast out devils and speak in new tongues and pick up serpents."

When he didn't go on Winona said, "That is all? Serpents? Does it say poisonous serpents?"

"No."

"Does it say rattlesnakes or some other kind of snake that can kill when it bites?"

"No and no."

"It just says serpents? But isn't the word 'serpent' another word for 'snake.'"

"Yes and yes."

"I still do not understand," Winona admitted.

"Some whites think it means poisonous snakes," Nate elaborated. "Maybe because the next part says that those who believe can drink any deadly thing and it won't harm them."

"Are you saying that some whites like to drink snake venom?"

Shakespeare chortled. "Not that I know of, but I wouldn't put it past a few lunkheads to try. But there are folks who think Mark is talking about poisonous snakes. So when they worship, they pick up rattlesnakes and copperheads and the like and handle them to show they have true faith."

"Please do not take this the wrong way," Winona said, "but whites are very strange."

"I know that better than anyone," Blue Water Woman said. "I live with a crazy white."

"Here now," Shakespeare said. "What did I do to deserve that? I'm as ordinary as butter."

Blue Water Woman looked at Nate. "Do you spend your whole day quoting a writer who died more winters ago than anyone can remember?"

"I do not," Nate said. "I think that would be silly."

Shakespeare turned red in the face.

"And you?" Blue Water Woman said to Samuel. "Do you go around quoting a dead man all day?"

"Heck no, ma'am," Samuel said. "To be honest, I can't read worth a lick. I couldn't quote one if I wanted to."

Blue Water Woman smiled at McNair. "I have made my point."

"How the blazes did we get on this subject?" Shakespeare complained.

Emala said, "I thought we were talkin' snakes."

The whole while, Nate had been prying at the head. He finally got it off and threw it away and stood. "I propose we organize a snake hunt. Shakespeare has lost a horse and I nearly got bit and my daughter nearly stepped on one, all since we got back."

"What about them?" Shakespeare asked with a nod at the Worths. "Weren't you fixing to raise a cabin?"

"Samuel and his family can stay with us," Nate said. "Tomorrow we hunt. The day after we'll start on their new home." He turned to the Worths. "That is, if you two don't mind?"

Emala took Samuel's big arm in hers. "Mr. King, we were talkin' about you last night and Samuel, he said you don't know how we feel about you, and now I see he's right. You surely don't."

"Feel how?"

It was Samuel who answered. "Do you know what it's like to be a slave?" He didn't wait for Nate to answer. "Of course you don't. You're white. But I was born a slave. Emala and me, both. We were told how to behave and where to live and what work we were to do. Our masters—that's what they called themselves and that's what we were to call them— our *masters* lorded it over us. We hardly had any say. I hated it. I hated it so much I had a powerful ache deep in me that wouldn't go away."

Nate listened with interest. He had known the Worths for a few months now, and this was the first time Samuel had gone into detail about their old life.

"I hated bein' made to do work I didn't want to do. I hated bein' made to live in a shack barely big enough for two people let alone four. I hated that I had to do what our masters said or I'd be whipped."

"How terrible," Winona interjected.

"You don't know the half of it, Mrs. King," Samuel said sadly. "But my point is this. I wanted out. I wanted a new life. I wanted to be a free man, to do as I please when I please. I wanted it with all I am. But I never became a runner. I wasn't sure we could survive."

"You've done fine if you ask me," Nate said.

"We've done fine thanks to *you*. You befriended us. You helped us against the slave hunters. You brought us across the prairie to the mountains. You said we could come live in your valley if we wanted and have a place of our own."

"You saved us," Emala said.

Nate didn't quite know what to say to that, so he said nothing.

"We owe you," Samuel said. "We owe you more than we can ever repay. So you want to wait a day to start our cabin? We don't mind. Hell, wait a month if you have to."

"What have I told you about swearin'?" Emala said.

"Not now, woman."

Nate said, "You don't owe me anything. I did the same for you as I'd do for anyone."

"That's another thing," Samuel said. "You look at us, you don't see the color of our skin."

"You don't know how rare that is," Emala said. "You don't know how special that makes you."

"I'm just me," Nate said.

"A fellow of infinite jest, of most excellent fancy,"

Shakespeare quoted. "He hath borne me on his back a thousand times."

"Enough about me," Nate said. "We have a problem and it has to be dealt with. Tomorrow we hunt snakes."

Chapter Four

Nate sent word to his son and the Nansusequas. By eight in the morning everyone in the valley was gathered at Nate and Winona's cabin. There were Zach and his wife, Louisa, Shakespeare and Blue Water Woman. There were the Nansusequas: Wakumassee, the father; Tihikanima, the mother; Degamawaku, their son; and their two girls, Tenikawaku and Mikikwaku.

The Worths were there as well. Samuel had offered to help, and Emala had said that of course they would but secretly she was more than a little afraid. She didn't like snakes. She didn't like snakes even a little bit. Now she and Samuel stood to one side as the rest talked and laughed, and the one thing she noticed, the one thing that struck her most, were all the guns. She had never seen so many guns on so few people in all her born days. All of them had rifles. Even the girls. Evelyn had what they called a custom-made Hawken. Teni and little Miki had rifles given to them by Nate and Winona. All the men wore at least two pistols. As did Winona, Evelyn and Blue Water Woman. Zach usually wore two, but for this occasion he had four wedged under his wide leather belt. Emala marveled that he didn't clank when he walked. Zach and his father and McNair also had big knives and tomahawks. Waku and Dega had knives. There were so many firearms and blades that at one point Emala turned to Samuel and said,

"Land of Goshen. Look at all the weapons. They could start their own army."

"Don't you dare say anything to them," Samuel cautioned. "They are our friends and I won't have you carpin'."

"Who's carpin', for goodness sake?" Emala rebutted. "All I'm doin' is tellin' you they have a heap of guns and whatnot."

"I aim to have my own heap before too long."

"What?"

"We each have rifles the Kings gave us. And I have a pistol. But that's all we have. As soon as we can, I am getting a rifle for Randa and Chickory and two pistols for each of you."

This was news to Emala. "We didn't need guns on the plantation."

Samuel gave her his look. "Are you addlepated, woman? They wouldn't let us *have* guns. They didn't want us risin' up against them." It was a subject dear to him. "When folks take it into their heads to lord it over other folks, the first thing they do is take away their weapons. You can't lord it over wolves. You can only lord it over sheep."

"I suppose that's true," Emala conceded. "But we aren't bein' lorded over anymore. What do we need with so many guns?"

"I want guns," Chickory said.

"Hush, boy," Emala said. "You're only fourteen. You are too young to be totin' an armory like that Zach King does."

"I want guns, too," Randa said.

Emala scrunched up her mouth as she had a habit of doing when she was displeased. "Listen to this. My whole family has gone gun crazy."

"It's not crazy," Samuel said. "It's practical. Out

here ain't like back at the plantation. We are in the wilderness now. The real wilderness. Not woods that have been tamed, like back there. Out here there are things that will kill us as soon as they smell us. Bears and those big cats and wolves."

"You're exaggeratin'. And we had bears and stuff back there, too."

"Black bears that were so scared of people they'd run off. Out here they ain't scared. And it's not just black bears. There are grizzlies. There are hostiles, too. Indians who won't care we're black and—what is it Nate calls it?" Samuel had to think. "Countin' coup. That's it. Indians like those Blackfoots. They'd kill us and rip off our hair."

"I haven't done the Blackfeet any harm," Emala said. "Why would they want to harm me?"

"Because you ain't one of them."

"That's hardly cause."

"Tell that to the whites who hate us because we're black. That ain't hardly cause, but they hate us anyway."

"Well," Emala said. It was the only thing she could think of to say, and that bothered her. Usually she could think of a lot more.

Nate came over. "Are you folks ready to hunt?"

"We are ready, Mr. King," Samuel said.

"Hopes the snakes are ready," Emala said.

"Excuse me?"

"Pay her no mind, Mr. King. She's in one of her moods. We've just been talkin' about how dangerous it is hereabouts and how we need weapons, and she thinks it's silly."

Nate smiled at Emala. "Your husband is right. This isn't like back East. You never know what you're going to run into. You can walk out the door one morning to fetch water from the lake and meet up with a griz. Or you can go for a ride with your daughter and come across a war party. You must always be prepared for the worst but hope for the best."

"I trust that the Lord will watch over us," Emala said.

"You take your faith seriously."

"You can bet your boots I do. Or your moccasins." Emala proudly held her head high. "I can read, Mr. King. I have my Bible and I read from it each and every day. And I trust in the Lord like the Bible says to."

"That's good," Nate said. "I trust in the Lord, too. But trust won't stop a hungry griz from eating you. Or an Apache or a Sioux from putting an arrow in you."

"Faith can move mountains," Emala said.

"This isn't about faith. It's about breathing. If you don't go armed, you won't be around for long."

"I don't know as I believe that."

"Emala," Samuel said.

"I mean, what are the odds of me walkin' out my door and there's one of those big bears or an Indian out to kill me? I bet it hardly ever happens."

"It only takes once," Nate said.

"We don't need a heap of weapons," Emala insisted.

Samuel gave her another of his looks. "Darn you, woman. Don't listen to her, Mr. King—"

"Nate. Please call me Nate."

"Don't listen to her, Nate. She is set in her ways. I want weapons. I want weapons for all of us. As soon as I can afford them."

"I've been thinking about that and I might have a way to help. We'll talk more about it later. For right now, our plan is to sweep the entire lakeshore from end to end. We'll each take a section. You and your family can start here and work north to Zach's. Zach is going to do the stretch from his cabin to Waku's lodge."

"We are honored to help."

Nate clapped Samuel on the arm and walked off and as soon as he was out of earshot Samuel turned to Emala.

"You are a trial."

"What did I do?"

"Arguin' with him like that. After all they have done for us."

"I was just speakin' my mind," Emala said. "Can I help it if I have a lot of mind to speak?"

"Enough. We have snakes to hunt."

"At last," Chickory said, and grinned. "I can't wait to bash a few." He hefted a log he had taken from the woodpile to use as a club.

Randa held up her hands. In each she held a fist-size rock. "If I can bean a rabbit on the hop I can surely bean me some snakes."

"Lordy," Emala breathed. "My family have become killin' fiends."

"Let's go," Samuel said, and moved toward the trees. "We'll spread out. We want to do this right so look under every rock. Every rattlesnake we find, we kill. If it's a big snake and you need help, give a holler. Just don't get bit."

They spaced themselves. Samuel was near the trees. Then came Chickory with his club and Randa with her rocks.

Emala, with her rifle, was by the lake. For some reason the weapon felt heavier than it usually did. She put her thumb on the hammer as Winona King had showed her how to do. She still didn't have the hang of loading. All that business about pouring the black powder and the patch and ball and the ramrod. Samuel always had to load for her.

Emala was glad to be by the lake. She figured there'd be fewer snakes near the water. She didn't know much about rattlesnakes, but she was pretty sure they didn't like water. Water moccasins did. Water moccasins terrified her. She remembered seeing one when she was little. She'd been six or seven and sitting on the bank of a pond when a water moccasin swam past. It scared her silly. She'd screamed and her ma snatched her up and backed away from the water moccasin, which paid no attention to them.

Emala checked on her children. Chickoy was looking under a rock. Randa was searching around some boulders.

Samuel looked at Emala and smiled. She smiled back, but she wondered what he was up to. He hardly ever smiled at her like that. He must want something, she decided. He was always nice to her when he wanted something. Men were sneaky that way.

Emala came to a cluster of rocks. Big rocks, middling rocks, little rocks. How they got piled that way was a mystery. She thought maybe the rising and falling of the lake might have something to do with it. Shakespeare had told her that sometimes the lake level rose when it rained real hard and that in the summer the level often dropped.

Emala poked at the rocks with her foot. A few clattered from the pile. She poked harder and a few more clattered. No snakes, though. She went to move on, then thought maybe she should sort through the whole pile. The Kings would. They were good people, the Kings. She liked them, liked them a lot.

She was grateful as grateful could be for them helping her family.

Emala shifted the rifle to her elbow and bent down. It was hard, bending. She was big across the hips and more plump than most women. She liked that word, "plump." She didn't like the word "fat." She had been plump ever since she could remember. "Plump as a peach," her mother would say. Or "Plump as a baked turkey." Emala liked being compared to a peach, but she wasn't so pleased about being compared to a turkey.

Something shot at her from the rocks.

Rearing back, Emala opened her mouth to scream. But it was only a bug. A brown beetle that scuttled swiftly away.

"Lordy," Emala breathed. Her heart was thumping. If it had been a snake she might have fainted. "I'm not cut out for this." She moved on. She had a job to do and she always did a job, any job, to the best of her ability. Whether she liked the job or not.

The others had gone farther than she had. She walked faster, careful not to misstep. She'd broke her leg as a girl and been wary ever since. Plump ladies didn't get around so good with broke legs.

Emala saw a flat rock about as big around as a cook pot. It didn't look very heavy, but when she pushed it with her shoe it wouldn't budge. Grunting from the effort, she bent and slipped her fingers under the edge and lifted. The rock wouldn't rise. That was good, she thought. There couldn't be a snake under there if it was wedged fast like that. She went to walk on and stopped. She wasn't doing the job right if she didn't look under it.

Emala set down her rifle. She gripped the edge with both hands and strained. The rock rose a little but not enough to see under. She strained again. She could feel drops of sweat trickling down her brow and down her arms. She wasn't fond of sweat. When it got in her eyes it stung.

"What are you doin', woman?"

Samuel was there. Chickory and Randa were well along the shore, searching.

"What does it look like I'm doin'?" Emala retorted. "I am lookin' for snakes."

"If you went any slower you would be a turtle." Samuel bent and lifted the flat rock with one hand. There was nothing under it but dirt.

"I can't help it if I'm not as fast or as strong as you."

"We can't be at this all day." Samuel straightened. "The rest of us will be done and you'll still be ploddin' along."

"I do not plod," Emala said.

Samuel shrugged and made toward the tree line. "Try to go faster. Give a holler if you need help."

As if Emala would. It made her blood boil, him treating her this way. Like she was next to worthless. She never heard him complain when she slaved over a hot stove to put food in his belly, or at night when she let him take what she liked to call his "liberties."

It was hard being a woman. Men didn't realize how hard. They didn't cook and sew and clean and give birth to babies. They didn't swell up and feel new life inside of them and go through hours or days of pain—she doubted a man could stand it. Women were tougher. That's why God let them have babies and not men. When it came to pain men were babies.

Emala grinned at the notion. Her grin became a chuckle and her chuckle a belly laugh.

"You all right over there?" Samuel called.

"Right fine," Emala replied between laughs. Just

because she was laughing, he thought something was the matter. Times like this, she wondered what the good Lord had in mind when he made men. Maybe he made them for women to laugh at. That made her laugh harder.

"What are you laughing at?" Samuel shouted.

"Silly things," Emala said.

Samuel muttered something and resumed searching for snakes.

Emala dabbed at her eyes and hefted her rifle and took a few deep breaths. "Lordy," she said in amusement. There were days when she amazed herself at how humorous she could be. She did so like to laugh. Her ma used to say it came natural to plump ladies, that skinny ladies were much too serious. Which always made Emala glad she was plump.

Grinning, Emala spied Zach and Louisa King way off on the north shore. She wondered if they were having as much fun as she was.

Chapter Five

"You shouldn't be doing this," Zach said for the tenth time since the hunt started.

"I'm with child," Louisa King replied. "I'm not helpless." She was small of frame with sandy hair she liked to crop short and eyes the same color as the lake. Usually she favored buckskins, but this past week she had taken an old brown homespun dress out of her trunk and was wearing that.

"Still, it's rattlers," Zach said. He was worried sick she'd be bitten; he could lose her and the baby both.

"I am not scared of snakes."

"That's your problem," Zach complained. "You're not much scared of anything."

"I was scared that time the army took you into custody and you were put on trial. I was scared I'd lose you."

"I'm still here," Zach said.

Lou sighed and turned and stared across the bright blue of the sunlit lake at the virgin valley beyond. She loved it here. Initially she had balked at moving from their old cabin in the foothills, but the move had turned out to be the smartest thing she ever did, next to marrying Zach. She liked the colors. She liked how the light green of the grass merged into the slightly darker green of the deciduous trees, the oaks and cottonwoods and willows, and how they, in turn, merged higher up into the even darker greens of the spruce and pine. Here and there stands of aspen were scattered. At this time of the year their leaves were a pale green, but in a few months they would flame with red and orange and yellow, the precursor of fall. Above the trees were high cliffs and jagged ramparts and crests crowned with snow.

A bald eagle soared over the valley on outstretched pinions, its predatory gaze on the ground. Several buzzards wheeled in concentric circles over woods to the east. In the water a streak of silver flashed clear and splashed down again.

"I hope we live here forever," Lou said.

"Could be we won't. Could be it will get as crowded here at it did along the front range."

"Crowded?" Lou teased. "We had five neighbors stretched out over twenty-five miles."

"For the Rockies that's crowded."

"You and your pa," Lou said, and laughed.

"What's that supposed to mean?"

"Only that you and your father love the wilderness. You can't stand to be hemmed in. It's a wonder you're not upset about the new people who have joined us. I don't mean just the Worths. I mean Waku and his family."

Zach hadn't been happy about it. His father tended to be too nice and offered sanctuary to anyone who needed it. If it had been him, he'd have told them to find a spot elsewhere.

Lou watched a pair of geese paddle majestically by. She liked how they held their heads high and moved along the water without hardly any movement of their bodies. "I think if I'd been born an animal I'd like it to have been a goose." She'd heard tell that geese mated for life. Feathered romantics, was what they were.

"That's plain silly." Zach never ceased to be amazed at the things that came out of her mouth.

"We should keep looking," Lou suggested. "We have a lot of shore to cover yet."

"I can do it alone," Zach tried again.

"If you were a horse you would have blinders on."

"Dang it, woman."

"I love it when you sweet-talk me."

Zach gave up. There was no reasoning with her at times. She got something into her pretty head and nothing could change it. And she *did* have a pretty head. As well as a pretty face and a pretty body and the prettiest smile of any female ever born. "Just be careful, all right?"

"Dang it," Lou imitated him. "Here I was hoping to give the first rattler we find a big hug."

"Ornery wench."

"Wench?" Lou repeated. "Did you just call me a *wench?* You've been hanging around Shakespeare too long."

Zach grinned.

Lou beckoned to the geese and said, "Quick! Come here and take a look! He has honest-to-God teeth!"

Zach laughed, and felt his worry lessen. She had that effect on him. She always seemed to know just what to do to make him feel good. "Don't tell anyone, but I love you."

"Oh my. Does this mean you have designs on me?" Lou grinned and patted her belly. "Oh. Wait. You already did have designs."

"You're hopeless," Zach said, and commenced to prowl among a jumble of rocks and boulders.

Louisa was pleased with herself. It took some doing to get him to not take things so seriously. Sure, he was serious by nature, but he had a wonderful sense of humor if he would only let it out more.

Lou came to a group of small boulders and carefully picked her way among them. She didn't dare slip. A fall might cause her to lose the baby. She smiled in anticipation. Her very own son or daughter. She hoped it was a girl, but Zach hoped it was a boy. She wished there were some way to tell. She had asked Winona and Winona said that her people believed that if a woman was carrying the baby high, it was likely to be a girl, and if she was carrying the baby low, it was likely to be a boy.

Lou looked down at herself. She had barely begun to show. It was much too soon to tell if she would carry high or low. Another few months maybe. She stepped around a knee-high boulder and over an ankle-high slab of rock and was within a few feet of the water's edge. She crouched and dipped her hand in and touched her wet hand to her neck and her forehead.

"What are you doing?" Zach asked from off a ways.

"Cooling off."

"Be careful you don't fall in."

Louisa looked at him to see if he was serious, and he was. As if by being pregnant she must be clumsy. A sharp retort was on the tip of her tongue, but she swallowed it. She dipped her hand in again and this time took a sip. Across the lake to the south was Shakespeare's cabin, figures moving near it.

Lou stood and wiped her right hand on her dress. With her rifle in her left hand she turned to catch up to Zach. She had to pass a couple of boulders that made her think of giant eggs. She was almost around them when a rattlesnake reared in a patch of shadow.

"Oh God," she blurted.

The snake was big and thick and its eyes seemed to bore into her with wicked intent. Its tail began to buzz.

Lou almost bolted, but the rattler was too close. She thought of the baby, and of how sick a bite would make her even if she didn't die. All that poison, it might harm the baby, might cause her to lose it. So she stood still, goose bumps breaking out all over.

The hideous head swayed in her direction.

Lou prayed that by not moving she wouldn't provoke it. She wanted to look to see if Zach had noticed, but she was afraid to even move her eyes. The snake might strike.

The buzz of its tail grew louder. For some reason the snake was becoming more agitated.

What could she do? She could try to shoot it, but it was bound to bite her before she got off a shot. She had heard they were lightning quick. And besides, she wasn't Zach. She couldn't shoot without aiming. In the time it would take her to take aim the snake could bite her three or four times.

All Lou could do was stand there and hope. She began to sweat. She hated when that happened. Sweat made her feel sticky, and she wasn't fond of how she smelled. *Please*, she inwardly prayed, *just go away and leave me be*. Their eyes met, or so it appeared to her, and a chill rippled through her clear to her toes. There was something awful, something alien about those eyes.

In her ears the buzzing rose to a crescendo. Although "buzzing" didn't quite fit. It was more like the rattle of seeds in a dry gourd. Its tail was sticking up in the air and vibrating fiercely.

Any moment now.

Lou resigned herself. It was going to strike. She must be ready and try to jump out of the way. She knew she would still get bitten but she had to try. She also knew that if she slipped and fell on the boulders, she might harm the new life taking form inside her.

The rattler's thick body was in an S, the head at the top of the S with the mouth parting.

This was it. Lou tensed and was on the verge of springing when the stock of a rifle flashed out of nowhere and struck the snake on the head with such force the reptile was flung against a boulder. It immediately started to coil and rear, but a moccasin-clad foot stomped on it just below the head, and the next thing, Zach bent and grabbed hold of the tail and began to swing the snake as if it were a rope. With each swing he smashed it against a boulder, again and again and again, smashing and smashing.

"Zach," Lou said.

Zach didn't hear her. He was making small animal sounds deep in his throat, snarls and growls as if he were a wolverine gone berserk. He swung and smashed and smashed some more so that the snake was turning to pulp.

"Zach?"

The snake was limp and had to be lifeless, but Zach suddenly slammed it down one more time and let go and drew his tomahawk. With a swift blow he separated the head from the body and then went on swinging, chopping the body to bits and pieces.

"Zach," Lou said, and put her hand on his arm.

Zach stopped chopping. He looked at her, his eyes wild with savagery and his lips curled back so that he looked as if *he* was about to bite her. His face was flushed with fury and he was breathing hard.

"I think it's dead."

Zach glanced down. He slowly straightened. The savagery faded from his eyes and he slowly became his usual self. He stared at the gore on his tomahawk. "I think you're right."

"I'll say one thing for you. When you kill a snake, you *kill* a snake."

"It was going to bite you," Zach said quietly.

"I know."

"I couldn't let it. I'll never let anything or anyone harm you so long as I'm breathing."

"No need to justify what you did." Lou gently squeezed his arm. "You did what you had to. You always do what you have to."

"That's what a man does," Zach said, and his voice was husky and almost hoarse.

"You do it well."

Zach coughed again, and set down his tomahawk and took her into his arms. "God," he said. "I almost lost you."

Lou snuggled against him. She was still holding her rifle and it was pressed between them and gouging her, but she didn't want to break the hug to set it down. She snuggled and kissed him on the neck, and said, "Thank you."

"Anytime."

"I know I can always count on you."

"It was ready to strike. If I'd come a second later . . ." Zach stopped.

"It's over."

"From this day on I'm killing every damn rattler I see."

"That's a little harsh, don't you think?"

"You might have died."

"You can't blame all snakes over this one. Another might have crawled off."

"I want you and the baby safe. So I mean it. Every rattler from now on is dead."

Lou snuggled and kissed his neck. "That's another thing I like about you. You don't do things in half measure."

"We should show it to my pa."

"Which piece?"

Zach started to laugh and caught himself. Lou started, and didn't stop. She let herself go. It felt good to laugh and feel the tension seep from her and leave her restored and happy. "I'm all right now."

"I lost control again," Zach said.

"You had cause."

"I told myself I would never lose control again, and I did."

"The important thing is that the snake is dead. Now we can get on with the hunt."

Zach let go of her and stepped back. "*I'll* go on with the hunt. *You're* going back to the cabin."

"We've been all through that. I'm not helpless. I'm taking part."

"No," Zach said firmly. "You're not."

Lou went to say that she was a grown woman and could do as she pleased, and looked into his eyes. "Oh," she said. "I guess I'm not."

Zach stepped to the lake and dipped the tomahawk in the water, swishing it until the gore was off, and wiped the tomahawk dry on his pants. Tucking it under his belt, he retrieved his rifle and held out his hand to her. "I'm sorry, but we can't risk the baby."

"No, we can't," Lou agreed.

"I'm sorry I lost control, too."

"Enough about that."

"I worry that one day I'll lose control and bring more trouble down on our heads, like I did with the army that time."

"Stop fretting. You were just being you. It's not the most important thing, anyway."

"What is?"

Lou turned to him. "Our love."

Chapter Six

"I think a rattlesnake just crawled up my leg," Shakespeare McNair remarked.

Nate was looking under a rock. "You're not half as humorous as you think you are." They had scoured most of the south shore and not come across a snake of any kind. He and McNair were near the grass, Winona and Blue Water Woman were over by the lake. They had been hunting for an hour now and would soon be at the east end.

"You think I jest, Horatio?" Shakespeare gave his right leg a vigorous shake and then bent as if to check if anything had fallen out. "I reckon you're right."

"Is this your way of saying my idea was a waste of time?"

"Not at all. Just last night I looked out my window and saw six rattlesnakes roll themselves into hoops and have a contest to see which of them could roll the farthest."

"You are a strange man."

Shakespeare put a hand to his chest as might an actor in a play. "I am giddy," he quoted. "Expectation whirls me around. The imaginary relish is so sweet that it enchants my sense."

"You have some?" Nate said.

About to go on, Shakespeare cocked his head. "Eh? I have some what? Snakes?"

"Sense."

"Oh my. A palpable hit. Yes, that is worthy of my

illustrious wife, who delights in sinking her verbal claws into my innocent flesh."

"Anyone would," Nate said.

"Ouch. Twice pricked," Shakespeare said indignantly. "I never realized how grumpy snake hunting makes some people."

Nate came to an old log and rolled it over. Nothing was under it. "I'm surprised we haven't found any."

"It could be there aren't any to be found. Or it could be they heard about your hunt and are lying up in fear somewhere."

"There must be a den," Nate said.

"Figured that out, did you?"

"Have you ever seen one? As old as you are, I bet you have."

"As old as . . ." Shakespeare stopped and puffed out his cheeks. "Were I a mongoose, I would bite you. I have never seen a snake den, no. I did have a friend who did, during the beaver days. His name was Franklyn. He kept seeing garter snakes go down this hole. His curiosity got the better of him and he dug at the hole until he found out why the garters were going down it."

Nate waited.

"According to Franklyn, he found a huge ball of them. Must have been hundreds. This was in the fall when they hole up for the cold weather."

"Hundreds?" Nate said.

"So Franklyn claimed. I had no cause to doubt him. He was a good man. Had a wife and a little one back home. Thought he'd save enough trapping beaver to give them a boost up in life."

"Was he good at it?" Nate had known men who tried their best but never were any good at skinning and curing.

"Very good, yes. He had about two thousand dollars on him the day the Blackfeet got him. Me and some others tracked them and found Franklyn in a clearing in the woods. They had staked him out and amused themselves chopping off his fingers and toes and ears. They'd cut his belly, too, and his guts were hanging out. He begged one of us to put him out of his misery."

"Let me guess. You did."

Shakespeare shrugged. "I never could stand to see anyone suffer. I made sure the money got to his family along with a note saying how he always talked about how much he cared for them." His features saddened. "The wife wrote me back. Thanked me for being so considerate and asked if I was in the market for a woman."

"She didn't."

"Not out plain, but it was there between the lines. Can't blame her, I guess. It would be hard raising children alone."

Nate stopped and placed his hands on his hips and surveyed the stretch of shore they had covered. "I reckon I was worried over nothing. There aren't all that many rattlesnakes around, after all."

"Better safe than bit."

"You're standing up for me? I figured you would poke fun from now until Christmas."

"Let's further think of this," Shakespeare quoted. "Weigh what convenience both of time and means may fit us to our shape if this should fail, and our drift look through our bad performance."

Nate shook his head. "I've put everyone to a lot of bother for nothing. It was coincidence, nothing more, those rattlers appearing so close together."

"If it had been two grizzlies or two mountain lions you'd have the same cause for concern."

"You can come right out and say when I'm wrong. I'm a grown man. I can take it."

"Oh, all right." Shakespeare quoted the Bard, "In the reproof of chance lies the true proof of men." He chuckled. "How's that?"

"You call that being hard on me?"

"Later I'll beat you with a switch if it will make you feel better."

"I've inconvenienced everyone."

Shakespeare put his hand to his chest again. "A true knight, not yet mature, yet matchless, firm in word, speaking in deeds and deedless in his tongue, not soon provoked nor being provoked, soon calmed. His heart and hand both open and both free."

"I'm no saint," Nate said gruffly.

"You're human. We all are. And as humans go, you are one of the few I have admired with all that I am."

"Why are you talking like this?"

"You never know," Shakespeare said.

Nate had a thought that troubled him. "This has something to do with your age, doesn't it? All you've done lately is talk about how old you are and how you don't feel as spry as you used to."

"I don't."

"Good God. You're over eighty. How spry do you think you should be?"

Shakespeare placed his hand on Nate's shoulder and said earnestly, "I'm preparing you, is all."

"Is there something you're not telling me?"

"No."

"You sick?"

"No."

"Have a disease of some kind?"

"No."

"Then why, for God sake?"

"I'm old, Nate. *Very* old. You keep denying how old I am. You tell me I'll last a good long while, but there are no guarantees. So I am saying now what I might not be able to say tomorrow or the next day."

"It might not happen for years yet."

Shakespeare shook his head. "I look at myself in the mirror every day and I know what I see." He sighed and raised his face to the vault of sky, then gazed at the lake. "I have no complaints. I've had a good life."

"Now you're being ridiculous. You act as if you have one foot in the grave when you've just admitted that you are as healthy as can be."

"Why doesn't anyone listen anymore?" Shakespeare said sadly. "My wife is denying my age just like you."

"I'll have Blue Water Woman and you over for supper tomorrow night and we'll talk some more."

"We'll be happy to come over, but I'll be damned if I'll be the topic. What I've just said to you goes no further than right here."

Nate grinned. "You just don't want Blue Water Woman upset with you."

"No. I don't want her upset, period. I love that woman, and talking about me dying would hurt her."

"You have my word," Nate said.

Winona looked up and saw her husband and McNair talking. "I thought we were hunting for snakes. Look at those two."

Blue Water Woman was using the butt of her rifle to move a large rock. "I hope it is not what I think it is."

Winona arched an eyebrow in a silent question.

"Shakespeare has been going on again about how no one lives forever," Blue Water Woman revealed. "He says he has a feeling, a premonition, that he isn't long for this world."

"Men can be so silly," Winona said. When her friend didn't respond, she said softly, "Blue Water Woman?"

Blue Water Woman turned. Her eyes were misting. "I am worried, Winona. It is all he talks about anymore. At first I thought it was his age. His joints hurt and he cannot get around as well."

"He gets around better than men half his age."

"You know that and I know that, but he says he is not the man he used to be. The other day he talked about how when he was younger he could swim a lake this size. Now he says he would be lucky to make it halfway across."

"Everyone grows old. It is part of life."

"It is part of dying," Blue Water Woman said. She walked to a boulder and sat. She rested the stock of her rifle on the ground and gripped the barrel in both hands and leaned on it. "In all the winters we have been together, I have never seen Carcajou like this."

Carcajou, as Winona knew, was a nickname given to Shakespeare in his younger days, before he discovered the Bard. It was French for "wolverine." Shakespeare never talked about how he got the name, not even to his wife.

"I tease him about it and he doesn't tease back," Blue Water Woman was saying. "That in itself worries me. It is as if a part of him has given up on living."

"Aren't you exaggerating a little?"

"No."

Winona sat on another boulder and placed her Hawken across her lap. "I have good ears if you want to talk about it."

"I know you do," Blue Water Woman said. "You are the best friend I have ever had." She bit her lower lip. "What I am afraid of is that Shakespeare is right. I could not live without him."

"We are getting ahead of ourselves," Winona cautioned. "When he shows more signs of his age than he has, then we should be concerned."

Blue Water Woman nodded bleakly.

"My people have a medicine we use in old age. We learned it from the Nez Percé. It is the seed of what the whites call the wild peony plant. You can chew it or drink it in a tea." Winona grinned. "Shakespeare need not know what the tea is for."

"You are a devious woman."

"Women have to be devious dealing with men. Men do not think as we do. They do not listen when we give them advice. They can be stubborn. And they have their pride."

"You do not need to tell me about pride. Shakespeare has enough for ten men."

"Men are like foals," Winona said. "They must be led. If we have to, we must trick them into thinking an idea is theirs when it is ours. When they balk, we must be patient, as we would with a foal, and coax and flatter them."

"Shakespeare does not take well to flattery," Blue Water Woman said. "He is too intelligent. He sees right through it."

"The same with Nate . . . most of the time," Winona said. "He is smarter than he gives himself credit for." She gazed over at the two men. They had stopped talking and were coming toward them. "Remember my offer of the tea."

"My people have a tonic, too . . ." Blue Water Woman said, and got no further. "Husband," she said, smiling at McNair. "We thought maybe you had stopped hunting."

"We thought the same about you." Shakespeare kissed her on the temple. "Saw you sitting over here. You must expect the rattlesnakes to crawl up and say, 'Here I am.'"

"We had one do that. Then it stuck its tongue out at us and crawled off laughing."

Winona linked her arm with Nate's. "Why so quiet? Something bothering you?"

"This hunt has turned into a waste of time. We should go see how Waku and his family are doing."

Waku and his family—and one other—were seated in the shade of a large spruce at the east end of the lake. The one other raised her arm and happily waved as Nate and the others approached.

"Do my eyes deceive me or is that fair young Evelyn sitting next to fair young Dega?" Shakespeare said.

"Evelyn offered to help them hunt," Nate detailed. "She told us it was the neighborly thing to do."

"Did she, now?" Shakespeare chuckled and nudged Winona with an elbow. "I trust I'll be invited to the wedding?"

"Husband," Blue Water Woman said.

Waku and his family hadn't found a single rattlesnake, Evelyn reported. Her arm was so close to Dega's that when she moved, she brushed against him.

Shakespeare turned and whispered in his wife's ear, "Isn't she the little hussy?"

"Husband," Blue Water Woman said.

Along about then Zach arrived. He told them of the snake that nearly bit Lou.

"But you killed it?" Nate said.

"It couldn't be any more dead, Pa."

Nate nodded and faced the rest. "I owe all of you an apology. We spent all this time looking, and for what? One measly rattlesnake."

"You did what you thought was right," Winona complimented him.

Shakespeare said, "I was hankering to stroll around in the hot sun anyway. I haven't sweated near enough this summer."

Blue Water Woman rolled her eyes.

Nate held his Hawken in his left hand and hooked his right thumb in his belt. "It wasn't a complete waste of our time. We know we don't have to worry about the rattlers. There are hardly any around."

In the gully to the northwest, in the underground chamber, the female who had recently mated was entwined in a writhing mass of sinuous forms. Other females had recently given birth and hundreds of little ones were exploring the den. In her dim way the female realized that never before had there been so many of them.

So very, very many.

Chapter Seven

In the days that followed, the rattlesnakes were largely forgotten. The folks in King Valley were busy with other things.

Nate asked the Worths to pick a site for their cabin. He rode with them around the lake, pointing out spots he thought were good, but he left the decision up to them. They made a complete circuit and when they were back where they started he drew rein and said, "Well?"

Samuel liked an area on the north shore midway between Zach and Lou's cabin and the Nansusequa lodge. It was flat and well back from the lake and in the shadow of tall spruce. He mentioned it, and Emala shook her head.

"What's wrong with it?"

"For one thing, I'd rather be closer to Winona. I like her. She's a fine lady and my friend."

"You can ride over to see her every day."

Emala fluttered her cheeks. "I'm not fond of sittin' a horse, thank you very much. Horses scare me. And plump as I am, it's a bother to climb on. I always have to ask you to help."

"I don't mind."

"That's not the point. I'd rather live where I can walk to Winona's cabin. It's more dignified."

Samuel surveyed the shore. "That means it would have to be between Nate's cabin and his son's or between Nate's and Mr. McNair's."

"How come you only mentioned the men?"

"What?"

"They have wives. You didn't mention Winona or Blue Water Woman or that darling little Louisa. Did you forget them?" It had been Emala's experience that men *did* tend to forget their womenfolk and needed to be constantly reminded of the love and devotion their women showed them.

"Good God."

"Don't blaspheme."

"I didn't forget them. I just didn't think to say them."

"That's the same thing." Emala put her hands on her hips. "You men. That we put up with you is a wonderment."

Samuel sighed and tilted his head back and stared at the sky.

"What are you doin'?"

"Countin' to ten."

"Don't you start with me, Samuel Worth. Let's walk along the lake and maybe I'll find a spot I like."

So that's what they did. They walked north. Samuel pointed out a suitable spot. Emala said it was too near the water.

"What's bad about that?" Samuel asked.

"Didn't you hear Winona? Sometimes it rains so hard the water rises. We don't want our home where it can be flooded."

Further on Samuel noticed a shaded spot near the trees.

"Too close to the woods," Emala said. "I could be out hangin' laundry and one of those big brown bears could jump out and gobble me up."

"Nate says there aren't any grizzlies in his valley. There was one, but he had to shoot it."

"It doesn't have to a grizzly that gobbles me. It could be a black bear. Or one of those tawny cats. Or a pack of wolves. Winona says sometimes at night you can hear them howlin' up on the mountain."

"They don't attack people all that often," Samuel had been told.

"I don't care. I won't be gobbled. I didn't come into this world to end up as some animal's supper. We'll have to find another spot."

Samuel stopped suggesting. They came to the northwest corner of the lake and Emala stopped to catch her breath. She saw where a giant pine cast a giant shadow and she went over to sit in the shade. A thicket fringed the woods to the right of the pine. To the left, a long stone's throw off, was what appeared to be a gully. "This is nice here."

Samuel scratched his head. "You said you didn't want a spot near the trees. This is closer than the place I picked."

"But it's nicer. There's all this shade. And it won't be easy for critters to sneak up on me with that thicket yonder."

"It's flat enough," Samuel said, and walked back and forth, examining the ground. He stared at the timbered slopes above and then at the lake. "It sure is pretty."

"It's near Winona, too." To Emala that counted for more. She liked to be around people. She liked to talk and laugh and sing. Samuel didn't. Back when they were slaves, he would as soon sit around their shack than gather at the fire with the other slaves and socialize. He stayed too much inside himself. She'd told him that a million times, but he stayed there anyway.

"All right. I'll go get Nate."

"Hold up. You're not leavin' me here alone." Emala heaved up off the ground. "Who knows what's lurkin' about?"

"You need to get over your fear," Samuel advised. "Otherwise you won't ever enjoy livin' here."

Emala regarded the towering peaks. She regarded the dark, somber forest and the high grass that could hide just about anything. "I can't help it. It's scary, and that's no lie."

"No more so than back at the plantation."

"What are you talkin' about? We didn't have bears out in the fields. We surely didn't have no wolves. And there weren't red men runnin' around wantin' to—what did Nate King call it?"

"Count coup."

"That's it. What is a coup, anyhow?"

"I didn't ask. But I don't think it's a thing. I think it's like hunters who shoot animals and put their heads on the walls."

"Whatever it is, it's not nice, and we didn't have none of it back home. So you can't blame—"

"No," Samuel said.

"No what?"

"The plantation was never ours. It wasn't our home. It was where we were forced to live, where we were treated the same as the horses and cows and sheep." Samuel gestured at the broad expanse of valley. "*This* is our home."

The sun was warm on Emala's face. She watched several geese come in for a graceful landing. A yellow and black butterfly fluttered past. Finches took wing, chirping gaily. "I guess it does have its nice parts." She took Samuel's hand. "I'll do the best I can, but it still scares me."

"I won't ever let anything happen to you."

They walked a ways and Samuel said, "I want to thank you, Emala."

"For what?"

"For stickin' with me through all of this. You've had to put up with a lot."

"Well, of course I'd stick with you. You're my husband. A wife is supposed to stick by her man, even when he's wrong."

"You think it's wrong we ran away? You think it's wrong I wanted a new life for us? A better life?"

Emala knew how important it was to him. More important than it was to her. She had been born a slave and never knew anything else. She had been used to that life. This idea of freedom, of doing what she wanted when she wanted, was almost as scary as the wilderness. "You weren't wrong," she said so as not to upset him.

Nate was at his new forge. He had built it several months ago out of rocks he collected along the lake. Nate had mixed the mortar, too, using clay and dirt and water. Shakespeare had offered to help and then sat and sipped blackberry juice Winona had made and kept pointing out that this or that stone wasn't set right and there were gaps in the mortar. It wasn't fancy, but it was the next best thing to having a blacksmith handy.

Nate built it mainly to shoe their horses. Not just his, but everyone else's in the valley. It didn't matter much to Winona or Blue Water Woman since the Shoshones and the Flatheads never shod their horses. Or to Shakespeare, who shod his mare only when he expected to ride long distances. It mattered to Nate, though. A lot of hard riding wore a horse's hooves down and could cause the animal a lot of pain. Shoes spared them from suffering.

The forge had a small bellows and an anvil, ordered out of a catalog at Bent's Fort. Ceran St. Vrain had sent word to Nate when they arrived and Nate had rigged an extrastrong travois to a packhorse to haul them back.

Now, standing under a plank roof supported by four thick poles, a precaution on Nate's part to protect his equipment from rain and snow, he picked up metal tongs and was about to grip a bar of wrought iron when Samuel and Emala appeared. They had been gone almost an hour and were walking hand in hand, the first instance Nate could recall them doing that. He walked hand in hand with Winona all the time. So did McNair with Blue Water Woman. As Shakespeare once joked, "We're natural-born romantic cusses."

"I hope we're not interruptin'," Samuel said.

Nate set down the tongs and came around the forge. "Not at all. What did you decide?"

Emala fanned her neck with her hand. "Land sakes, it's powerful hot under here. It's like standin' on the sun."

"The forge has to be hot or the metal won't melt," Nate said.

"We found us a spot," Emala told him. "We'd like for you to come have a look-see and tell us what you think."

Nate undid his apron and set it aside. He took his Hawken from where he had propped it. "Show me."

They headed north along the lake. Nate held his Hawken with the barrel across his shoulder, his hand on the stock.

Emala nodded at the rifle. "You don't go anywhere without that, do you, Mr. King?"

"It's Nate, remember? And no, not if I care to go
on breathing."

"Those things are too heavy for me. My arms get
tired. I'd rather go without."

"You get used to it."

Emala regarded the wooded slopes high above. "I
wonder if I'll ever get used to any of this."

"It's our home," Samuel said.

"So you keep remindin' me. But not yet it ain't. Not
until I have my very own cabin. Which reminds me,
how's that goin' to work, exactly, Mr. King? I mean,
Nate?"

"We will all pitch in and help build it," Nate explained. "Raising a cabin, it's called."

"I never been to one of those."

Nate noticed a pair of doves in flight. He had always liked doves. His uncle once told him that when
they mated it was for life. If one or the other died, the
survivor never took another. He never did learn
whether that was true.

"Mr. King?"

Nate glanced over. Samuel was studying him, his
brow furrowed. "What's on your mind?"

"I've been meanin' to ask you somethin' and I
suppose now is as good a time as any."

"Ask away," Nate said.

Emala had an inkling what her husband was cu-
rious about. They'd talked about it just the night before. "Maybe you shouldn't."

"Why not?" Samuel asked.

"People put out a hand to help, you should accept
it and that should be that," Emala said.

Nate asked, "What is this about?"

"You. Your wife. Your family. Your friends," Samuel ran off a list. "But mostly you and your wife."

"What did we do?"

"That's just it," Samuel said. "What *haven't* you done? From the moment we met you, you folks have treated us kindly and gone out of your way to do us favors."

"For which we're grateful as can be," Emala said.

"That we are," Samuel concurred. "When we first met you all we had was the clothes on our backs, and you bought us new clothes and gave us guns and protected us all the way here."

"Your point?" Nate was unsure what they were leading up to.

"My point is a question," Samuel said. "What I would like to know is *why*. Why did you and your wife do all those things? And why are you still goin' out of your way to help us?"

"Because you needed our help then, and you need our help now," Nate answered.

"But we were strangers. More than that, we're black and you're white. We're used to whites lookin' down their noses at us, not treatin' us as equals. I thought you were up to somethin' but you weren't. You were just bein' you."

"I was being me when I took Winona for my wife. You might have noticed that she's not white, either."

"So skin means honest-to-God nothin' to you?"

"It's not a person's color, it's the person inside," Nate said. "Winona isn't white, but she's the most beautiful woman I've ever known. I love her more than I love anything."

Nothing more was said until they came to the spot Emala had picked. Nate walked in a circle and said, "There's plenty of flat ground for a good-size cabin, and you're close enough to the lake that it won't be too much of a chore fetching water."

"What about that?" Emala nodded toward the gully. "Do we need to worry it will flood if it rains heavy?"

Nate shook his head. "Even if it does, your cabin will be far enough away to be safe." He smiled and nodded. "I think you've chosen a fine spot for your new home. You shouldn't have any problems at all."

Chapter Eight

The cabin raising got underway.

First the flat area was cleared of rocks and everything else. Nate and Shakespeare measured and pounded stakes at the four corners and strung rope between the stakes as guidelines. The foundation stones were laid. Then came the felling of the trees. Cottonwoods and firs were too slender. Spruce was scattered here and there near the site, and there were plenty of oaks, but the tree Nate liked best were pines. Pines were abundant and there were enough of them near the same size.

Nate and Shakespeare and Zach all owned axes. Nate owned two, and lent his extra to Samuel. Nate picked a cluster of trees and set to work. With each stroke his ax bit deep and sent chips flying.

Shakespeare was an old hand at felling trees, and Zach had learned from his father.

Samuel had never used an ax in his life. On the plantation most of his work had been in the cotton fields, and you didn't chop cotton with an ax. He watched them, then imitated what they were doing. He soon found it wasn't as easy as they made it seem. He swung hard enough, but his ax didn't go in as far and he wasn't making much headway.

A hand tapped him on the shoulder.

"Watch me," Nate said. He showed how to grip the ax and how to swing at an angle so the blade penetrated. "You turn your hips as you swing and put your shoulders into it."

Samuel tried it a few times and smiled at his improvement. "I'm obliged," he said.

Nate wasn't done. "Another thing is that when you pull the ax back, don't jerk it. Swing and pull back smoothly the moment the ax has gone in as far as it will go. That way you don't jar your body and wear yourself out. It's a steady motion." He demonstrated. "See?"

"Let me try." Samuel stepped to the trunk and planted himself and swung. The ax became wedged and he had to tug to work it free. "What did I do wrong?"

"You swung too hard. Take easier strokes and let the ax do most of the work."

It wasn't long before Samuel got the hang of it, but once he did he went at it with fierce desire. These were the logs for his new home and he couldn't wait to have it done.

Tree after tree crashed down. The women and Evelyn and the Nansusequas used hatchets to trim the branches and threw them into a pile.

Shortly before noon Winona and Blue Water Woman and Lou stopped trimming to set out the midday meal. Blankets were spread, as if it were a picnic, and food they had prepared the night before was placed on the blankets. There was venison and potatoes and green beans and carrots, plus a pie Lou had baked.

The Nansusequas had brought rabbit stew. Waku and Dega came to Nate and offered to hunt meat for the supper pot and Nate said that would be a great help. He was resting on a stump. Winona walked over with a glass of water and smiled and handed it to him.

"You look thirsty."

Nate was sweating from head to toe. "I could drink the lake dry," he boasted.

Evelyn joined them and asked, "Do you need me for anything?"

"You can help trim more branches when the men go back to work," Winona said. "Why do you ask?"

"I'd like to go hunt with Dega."

Nate lowered the glass. "You?"

"What's wrong with that?"

"You want to *hunt?*"

A pink tinge crept into Evelyn's cheeks. "Yes. Me. We have to eat, don't we?"

"You've never liked to kill," Nate reminded her. Yet recently she had gone off to the prairie after buffalo with the Nansusequas. Now this.

"I get hungry the same as everyone else."

"Are you sure that's the only reason you want to go?"

The pink in Evelyn's cheek darkened to red. "What else would there be, Pa?"

Winona interceded with, "You go right ahead, Daughter. Waku and Dega are waiting."

Evelyn grinned and kissed her mother on the cheek and spun and hurried off giggling.

Nate upended the glass and smacked his lips. "Right considerate of you to fuel their fire."

"I do not see flames anywhere."

"Cute," Nate said. "It surprises me, is all, you letting her go off with him. At this rate they'll want a cabin of their own inside of a month."

"She is young and in love. Were I to deny her, she

would sneak around and see him behind our backs. Is that what you want?"

"I hope we've raised her better than that."

"The heart wants what the hearts wants," Winona said. "The best we can do is guide her."

Nate wasn't entirely sure he approved. He liked Dega. The boy had many fine qualities. But he didn't see Evelyn as ready for such a big step. He watched her walk off, both she and Dega smiling broadly. His daughter—in love. He could hardly believe it.

The work resumed. Horses were brought, ropes were rigged, and the logs were dragged to the site. They had to skirt the gully each time; it was directly in the way. Once, as Nate was guiding a claybank pulling a log, he thought he glimpsed a snake. He almost stopped to look for it but remembered his folly of the snake hunt and went on by.

For two days they felled and trimmed and hauled large pine after large pine. The logs were laid out in rows. Nate and Shakespeare then went from one to the next, notching them. The notches had to be cut just right. Too shallow, and the logs wouldn't fit snug. Too deep, and the ends tended to weaken over time.

Samuel drank it all in. He asked if he could notch a few and Nate showed him how. He got the first notch done and stood back.

"How did I do?"

Nate inspected it. "Right fine."

"I hope you don't mind that I want to help. You know why it's important to me, don't you?"

"Yes."

"If there is ever somethin' I can do for you . . ." Samuel didn't finish.

"No need," Nate said.

"As much as I respect you, there is. You've treated me more decent than anyone on this earth. I would die for you if I had to."

Nate chuckled and clapped Samuel on the back. "Let's hope it doesn't come to that."

"I'm serious, Mr. King. I keep bringin' this up because you don't realize what it means to me and my family. We have a place to live, thanks to you. We'll have a new home, thanks to you. Most of all, we're free, thanks to you and Winona. *Free*, after all those years as slaves." Samuel bowed his head and coughed. "I have wanted my freedom more than I have ever wanted anything. I dreamed of it when I worked in the fields. I dreamed of it at night. To finally have my dream come true . . ." He coughed again.

It gave Nate a lot to think about. That night, as he lay weary but content in his bed with Winona's cheek on his shoulder and her hair tickling his ear, he remarked, "I like that Samuel Worth. He's a good man at heart."

"He is like someone else I know," Winona said.

"Touch the Clouds?"

Winona laughed and poked him in the ribs. "My cousin is a good man, too, but he is not as good as you."

"I bet Blue Water Woman would say the same about Shakespeare and Lou about Zach and Tihi about Waku."

"They would, yes. But you are special."

"How so?"

Winona kissed him. "You are *mine*."

It was a while before they got to sleep. Nate slept well and woke before dawn. He carefully eased out from under Winona's arm and slipped out of bed.

Rising, he stretched, then went through his morning ritual of donning his buckskins and powder horn and ammo pouch and possibles bag and going outdoors to heed nature's need.

The sky was still dark. Stars sparkled in the firmament. A strong breeze stirred his hair. He breathed deep of the smell of the lake and the dank scent of the nearby forest and listened to the hoot of an owl. Instead of using the outhouse he walked around to the corral and heeded nature there while checking that the horses were all right. Of late they had been acting up. He suspected a mountain lion or maybe a bear, although he had not seen sign of either.

Nate yawned and shook his head to clear the cobwebs. He went to the lake. The water was tranquil. He dipped his hand in and splashed some on his face. Somewhere a goose honked, as if startled. He remembered when Zach and Evelyn were little and he taught them to fish. Evelyn hated it. As he recollected, she called fish "icky" and never did develop a taste for fish meat. Neither did he. He much preferred succulent venison or juicy buffalo meat or the tastiest meat of all, cougar.

Rising, Nate turned to go back to the cabin. He took two steps. Directly in front of him something hissed. He froze, suspecting a snake. The rattling of the serpent's tail proved him right.

Not many people knew that rattlesnakes did most of their hunting at night. This one was after prey—and Nate had almost stepped on it. Try as he might, Nate could barely see the thing. It wasn't big, but it wasn't a rattlesnake's size that mattered—it was their venom. He held himself still except for his hand, which he inched toward his belt. His fingers brushed leather and he nearly gave a start. He had done something he hadn't done in years; he had come outside without his pistols. Anger flared. If he had told the kids once he had told them a thousand times to never, ever make that blunder, and here he had done it himself. He didn't have his rifle or his tomahawk either. All he had was his Bowie, and only because the sheath was attached to his belt.

Nate eased his hand to the hilt of the big knife. He began to slowly draw it out.

The snake's head rose like a black stick and the rattling grew louder. It was preparing to strike.

Nate debated trying to spring aside. He was quick, but rattlesnakes were quick, too. He almost had the knife out.

Suddenly the snake stopped rattling. Its head dropped and it slithered swiftly away toward some rocks.

Whipping the Bowie high, Nate went to throw it but changed his mind. He had practiced until he could hit the center of a target consistently at about ten feet. But the snake would be a lot harder to hit and he might damage the blade. Instead, he skirted the rocks and went inside. He would deal with the rattler when the sun came up.

Nate rekindled the fire in the fireplace. He had been toying with the notion of buying Winona a stove. The catalog at Bent's Fort listed a new kind made all of metal. They weighed a lot and it would cost dear to have it shipped west from St. Louis, but he thought it might make a nice surprise. From what he had heard, ladies back in the States loved them.

He went to the cupboard and took down the coffee tin. He filled the pot with water from a bucket on the counter, and took the pot to the fireplace. From another cupboard he helped himself to a corn dodger and sat in the rocking chair and nibbled while the coffee heated.

Another rattlesnake. Nate told himself it was nothing to be bothered about. Rattlesnakes were as common as rabbits. Most years, he would spot a few. Unless they were close to his cabin he usually left them alone. That there were so many of late was troublesome, but after the fiasco of his hunt, he figured he wouldn't make an issue of it.

The dodger was delicious. Winona had learned to make them just for him, and she added honey to the cornmeal. No sooner did he think of her than the bedroom door opened and out she came tying the purple robe he had bought for her.

"Tsaangu beaichehku."

It was Shoshone for "good morning." *"Tsaangu beaichehku,"* Nate replied, drinking in her beauty. He never tired of looking at her, of being with her. That she cared for him as deeply as he cared for her was a gift beyond measure. "Sleep well?"

"Haa."

Shoshone for "yes." "We are speaking your tongue today, I take it?" Nate said.

Winona smiled and ran a hand through her hair. She padded in her bare feet over to the rocker and bent and kissed him lightly on the lips. "We can speak whichever tongue you want, husband."

"We'll speak yours, then. It embarrasses me that you speak mine better than me."

Winona rubbed her fingers over his beard. She loved to do that. As she loved to feel his muscles and to listen to him breathe in the quiet of the night. "I will fix breakfast." She moved to the counter. "How soon do you go off to chop more trees?"

"I'm supposed to meet Shakespeare about an hour after sunup. Should give me enough time."

"For what?"

Nate told her about the rattlesnake.

In the act of smearing grease in a pan, Winona looked up. "Why not let it be?"

"Can't."

"I have never known you to make such a fuss over snakes. It reminds me of Lame Bear."

"Isn't he that old man who can hardly walk? Kin of yours on your mother's side?"

"He is the one, yes. With him it is flies. He goes around the village killing all the flies he can."

"Are you saying I'm feebleminded?"

Winona smiled sweetly. "Not yet. But you are working on it."

Chapter Nine

Nate didn't find the snake. He poked among the rocks and turned over some of the larger ones, but it was gone. In annoyance he kicked the ground and then headed for the cabin site.

Shakespeare and Zach were already there and Shakespeare was regaling the Worths with a tale of his early years. McNair winked and grinned at Nate and went on with his story.

"So there I was, all alone in Blackfoot country in the cold of winter with the snow so deep only a few treetops showed and—"

"Wait a minute," Randa said. "Are you tryin' to tell us the snow was so deep it buried the *trees?*"

"Oh, come now, Mr. McNair," Emala said.

Samuel and Chickory both grinned.

"Believe it or not, ladies," Shakespeare responded. "I'll have you know that I am a veritable fount of veracity."

"A what?" Randa asked.

"It means he always tells the truth," Nate explained, "except when he opens his mouth."

The Worths all laughed.

Shakespeare feigned indignation. "Your fine wit, Horatio, is something stale and hoar ere it be spent."

"Was that that dead guy you always talk like?" Chickory asked. "It sounded peculiar like this talk does."

Nate smothered a laugh of his own.

"Yes, that was William S.," Shakespeare answered. "The finest scribe who ever drew breath."

Emala said, "Go on with your story. That other fella I can't hardly ever understand."

McNair cleared his throat. "Very well. So there I was, alone in Blackfoot country, with snow and ice everywhere. The Blackfeet had taken my horse and my pack animal and I was stranded afoot. I had to walk out. I'd gone about ten miles in the fifty-below weather when—"

"Wait a minute," Randa interrupted again. "Did you say fifty *below*?"

"Why, Mr. McNair, nothin' is ever that cold," Emala said.

"I will have you know, madam, that in some parts of the north country it does, indeed, get that cold, and colder. With the wind blowing it can easily reach seventy-five below."

"Land sakes. The tales you tell," Emala said.

"Go on," Samuel urged.

McNair cleared his throat again. "So anyway, I came to a river that was frozen over and—"

"Which river?" Chickory asked.

"What?"

"Which river was it?"

"I don't know as it even had a name. A lot of rivers back then didn't and many still don't. But if it's a name you need, some of the Indians called it the Sweet Grass River."

"Why did they call it that?" Randa asked.

"Because it cut through the prairie, I believe," Shakespeare said with a trace of exasperation. "The name isn't important. The important thing is what happened when I tried to cross it. You see, it had frozen over, but when I was about halfway across the ice crackled and started to break just like—"

Emala held up a hand. "Hold on. You told us it was fifty below. Why, mercy me, that ice had to be five feet thick. How could it crack?"

"It just did."

"But you don't weigh all that much and back then you were likely skinnier. Am I right?"

"Yes, you are, but you see—"

Emala shook her head. "No. It don't hardly seem possible. But go on with your story if you want."

"Thank you." Shakespeare sighed. "I was in the middle of the river and the ice started to crack. I tried to run, but the ice was too slippery and I kept falling. Just when I thought I might make it, down I went. I managed to catch hold of the edge of the ice with my arms but I lost my rifle and it sank out of sight and—"

"You must have been powerful cold," Randa said.

"It's a miracle you didn't freeze solid," Emala mentioned.

"I might have," Shakespeare acknowledged. "But just then a grizzly happened by and spotted me dangling there. I was scared to death, as you can imagine. I was even more scared when he came over and sniffed me and—"

"Wait a minute," Randa said. "The ice was thick enough to hold one of those giant bears, but it wouldn't hold you?"

"It came from the shore side where the ice was thicker," Shakespeare said. "I was out in the middle. Anyway, it sniffed me a few times and then opened its mouth and I figured I was a goner. I expected it to chomp on my head and that would be the end of me. But—"

"What was its breath like?" Chickory asked.

"What?"

"Its breath. Dog breath always stinks. I bet bear breath stinks even worse. Did it make you gag?"

Shakespeare looked at Nate and Nate pretended to be interested in some clouds.

"I was too scared to pay much attention. All I remember is its teeth and how I thought I was doomed, when lo and behold, that griz went and bit down on the back of my shirt and lifted me right out of the water and dragged me in to shore."

"Let me guess the end of your story," Samuel said. "It dragged you to shore and ate you."

Emala and the children tittered and cackled.

"I am done," Shakespeare declared.

"No. Please," Emala said. "We want to hear the rest. What happened next? How did you get away?"

"I think the best grace of wit will shortly turn into silence, and discourse grow commendable in none only but parrots," Shakespeare quoted.

"I don't know what any of that meant," Emala said.

"Maybe I'll finish my tale later. We have a lot of work to do."

"Now you've done it," Emala said to Samuel. "You've hurt his feelings."

Everyone got busy. Nate stripped to the waist and went in among the trees with his ax. Today they needed logs to use as ceiling beams. The logs had to be not only big but strong enough to support the weight of a heavy snowfall.

McNair tagged along, muttering to himself.

"Something the matter?"

"I am feeling old and grumpy."

"Maybe you should have told them about the time you rode an elk. It's more believable."

"I did, consarn you. On a dare." Shakespeare rubbed his white beard. "I was young and stupid in those days."

"I saw another rattlesnake this morning," Nate said.

"Imagine that. In the wilderness, no less."

"Have you come across any since the hunt?"

Shakespeare shook his head. "I don't make it a point to look. I'm not as fond of them as you are."

A stand of oaks drew Nate's interest. Several were more than thick enough. He patted a trunk. "What do you think?"

"That there isn't enough respect in this world for those with white hair."

"I meant the trees."

"Oh." Shakespeare walked around it. "Nice and straight. And oak is stronger than pine."

"Let's do it."

Shakespeare nodded and chose another.

Nate settled into a rhythm, swinging smoothly and powerfully. Chips flew with each bite of his ax blade. When the oak gave a lurch and there was a loud *crack,* he yelled, "Timber!" and quickly backed away. With a tremendous boom, the giant oak fell. It took a few smaller trees with it and when it hit, raised bits of grass and dust into the air.

A few minutes later the tree Shakespeare had picked came crashing down. He walked over, his brow glistening with a sheen of sweat. "That felt good."

"See," Nate said. "You're not as old as you keep saying."

"Because I can chop down a tree?"

"You never once stopped to rest. Many men would have."

"I have never been puny," Shakespeare said. He gazed about them at the untamed wilds. "You can't be and survive out here."

"Neither puny nor careless," Nate said.

Evelyn appeared, carrying a pitcher and two glasses. She was wearing one of her best dresses and a bonnet Nate had never laid eyes on before. He had seen her sewing something a few days ago and now he knew what. "That's new," he said, nodding.

"Yes," Evelyn said absently.

Shakespeare studied it. "I've never seen you in a bonnet, young one. It becomes you."

"I'm not so young anymore," Evelyn replied in the same absent tone, "and I was hoping it would."

"You act down in the dumps," Shakespeare remarked.

Evelyn gave a toss of her head and smiled. "Sorry. It's just that Dega isn't here today."

Nate and Shakespeare exchanged covert glances.

"Not here?" Nate said.

"No. He's off with his pa, hunting. His sister says he wanted to come but Waku promised you he would do the hunting and Dega had to go with him."

"It's rough having a stomach," Shakespeare said.

Evelyn blinked and then grinned. "You say the strangest things, do you know that?"

Nate said, "You'll get to see Dega later probably."

"I hope so." Evelyn gave each of them a glass. "I brought blackberry juice. Ma made it as a surprise."

"Daisies and nags rolled into one," Shakespeare said.

"Excuse me?"

"Women," Shakespeare said.

"That's awful. Not all women nag, I am sure."

"Girl, you're, what, sixteen? You've lived long

enough to know that females will be females and males will be males and never the twain shall meet."

Shakespeare chuckled. "Well, except under the blan—"

Nate nudged him with an elbow, hard.

"Except what?" Evelyn asked.

"Except in the heart, where it counts the most," Shakespeare said, and rubbed his side. "If it wasn't for love we'd likely kill each other off."

"Love," Evelyn said dreamily.

Nate wagged his glass. "Are you going to pour or do we do it ourselves? I'm right thirsty."

"Sorry, Pa."

Shakespeare waited his turn, took a long sip, and smacked his lips in satisfaction. "Delicious. Tell your ma if I wasn't married to my personal nag and she wasn't hitched to this lunkhead next to me, I'd dang well propose to her."

"I'll tell my ma no such thing," Evelyn said. "You're terrible."

Shakespeare drank more juice and said, "Marriage isn't a bed of roses, fair maiden. You'd do well to remember that."

"But you believe in love. You just said so."

Shakespeare smiled and said kindly, "Yes, precious. I believe in love as much as I believe in anything."

"Me, too. I think about it a lot."

Shakespeare took another sip and looked at a pair of finches that flew past and then at the sky and then at his moccasins and then he said, "Have anyone in particular in mind when you think about love?"

"Who? Me?"

"I wasn't talking to Horatio, here. I already know he loves Winona. The wisest choice he ever made in his whole life." Shakespeare raised his glass and stared at her over the rim. "How about you?"

"I'm too young to be in love."

"Really?"

Nate bit his lower lip to keep from laughing.

"And even if I was, I wouldn't talk about it," Evelyn said defensively. "Love is personal and private."

"Do tell."

"It's true. When we talk about it, we spoil it."

"I never knew that."

"Unless it's with the one we love. Then it's all right to talk about it. Sort of like heart to heart."

"I will be sure to mention that to Blue Water Woman. We have been making a spectacle of ourselves talking about our love in public."

"You're teasing, aren't you?"

"Perish forbid," Shakespeare said, and launched into a quote. "With love's light wings did I o'er-perch these walls, for stony limits cannot hold love out, for what love can do, that dares love attempt."

"What are you saying? That it is all right to talk about our special love with just about anybody?"

"There is talking and there is talking. But you are right, princess. There are things we talk about with those we love that we wouldn't say to total strangers."

"Are you teasing again?"

"Never about the shrine we hold most dear. That is, if we are talking about the same shrines."

"I'm so confused," Evelyn said.

Nate drained his glass and handed it to her. "Tell your mother we'll be trimming a while. And don't ever come into these woods again without your rifle."

Evelyn was reaching for Shakespeare's glass, and

stopped. "I had the pitcher and glasses to carry. Besides, I have my pistols and my knife. And I heard you chopping and knew you weren't far."

"Never ever," Nate said.

Frowning, Evelyn took the glass and wheeled on her heels. "I'm not a child. I can take care of myself."

"Blue Flower," Nate said sternly, using her Shoshone name.

Evelyn glanced over her shoulder.

"I don't want to have to bury you."

She walked on without saying a word.

A gust of wind stirred the trees and farther in the forest a raven squawked.

"It has long amused me," Shakespeare said, "that when we are young we think we know everything and when we are old and look back we realize we didn't know much of anything. She's growing up, Horatio. She has a mind of her own."

"Doesn't make it easier."

"No, the older they get, the harder it is. But look at the bright side."

"I shudder to ask," Nate said.

"In a year or so you might be a grandpa."

Chapter Ten

The chickens needed to be shooed in at dusk. Bob-cats and foxes and coyotes and wolves loved to gorge on chicken flesh.

It was Evelyn's job. Or, as she preferred to think of it, her chore. She didn't much like chickens. When they were fresh out of the egg they were adorable. They chirped sweetly and looked so cuddly she always wanted to pick them up. But as they aged they lost their cuteness and would often as not peck anyone who tried to handle them.

When her pa first got them there were ten, but now there were eighteen, counting the rooster. Evelyn liked him, liked how he strutted around with his chest puffed out and put on displays for the hens. She didn't like how he crowed each morning at the crack of day and woke her. She would as soon sleep in.

On this particular evening, most of the sun had been devoured by the maw of hungry night. Evelyn had herded eleven of the chickens inside the coop but couldn't find the rest. She went toward the lake and spied five close to the water. One was a big hen she called Matilda. Matilda thought she was a rooster. She had her own little band that followed her everywhere and did whatever Matilda did.

"There you are," Evelyn said as she slowly circled to get behind them so they couldn't run off. They clucked and Matilda dug at the dirt and flapped her wings. "It's time for bed." Evelyn waved her arms. "Get going."

Matilda in the lead, they moved toward the coop. They took their time, as they always did, in no rush to be locked in.

Evelyn stamped her foot in irritation. "Faster, darn you. I am meeting Dega later and have things to do." A secret meeting, as they had been doing for a while now. She would tell her folks she was going to bed and slip out her window and spend an hour or so with him and slip back in again with her parents none the wiser.

Evelyn never imagined there would come a day when she would do anything so brazen behind their backs. She loved and respected them. She truly did. But she doubted they'd approve and might even try to stop her, and she couldn't have that. Dega meant too much to her. The thought made her cheeks grow warm. She hadn't been honest with Shakespeare. She wasn't too young to be in love. She had, in fact, been in love for some time and not realized it until recently. Peculiar how the heart worked, she reflected. Even more peculiar that the mind sometimes denied what the heart was feeling. She had denied hers until her feelings for Dega washed over her in a tidal wave of desire.

A short ramp led to the floor of the coop, which was raised off the ground about a foot. Matilda led her group up it and flapped her wings again before entering and gave Evelyn a look that suggested were it up to Matilda she would spend her nights outside, thank you very much.

Evelyn shut the small door but didn't latch it. Not yet. There were two chickens unaccounted for. It didn't help that their feathers were reddish brown. It made them hard to see in the murky twilight.

Evelyn went around the cabin to the corral, where the chickens liked to bathe in the dust, but the missing chickens weren't there. She walked to the rear of the cabin, where the chickens liked to peck at the tiny stones, but the missing pair weren't there either. She moved to the other side. Still no chickens.

Puzzled, Evelyn scanned the lakeshore and the tree line. Usually they didn't wander far. Some instinct kept them close.

Evelyn knew which chickens were missing, two of the smallest. They had hatched at the same time and always went everywhere together. Sometimes they were with the rooster and sometimes with Matilda, and other times they wandered by themselves. She roved the shore for fifty yards and retraced her steps and went the same distance in the other direction. She crossed to the woods and moved along the border for a considerable distance.

"Where did you get to, consarn it?" Evelyn asked the empty air. She had other chores to do and she wanted to wash up before she pretended to turn in and went out her window to be with Dega. The thought of him, of his wonderful eyes and his handsome face, sent a tingle down her spine. *Who would have thought,* she asked herself, *that I would ever feel this way?* When she was younger she had known beyond any shadow of doubt that she was never going to fall in love and never going to marry. She had felt no need for a man and never had a hankering to have children and a family. Yet here she was, in love, and the notion of a family of her own pleased her mightily.

"Life," Evelyn said, and grinned. She sure had

learned a lot about herself in the past several months. It was a mild shock to learn she was so changeable. She thought she knew herself inside and out, but it turned out she didn't know herself at all. How that could be was a mystery. If people didn't know themselves, how could they know anyone else?

Evelyn shook her head. She was tired of thinking about it. She returned to the cabin and stood near the corral tapping her foot in impatience. The two chickens had to be somewhere. She wondered if maybe they were already in the coop.

The world around her was gray fading to black as Evelyn knelt and opened the door and peered in. She couldn't make out much, but she could smell the chickens and the straw and droppings. She lowered the door and rose. "They have to be in there," she said to herself. But if she were wrong and the chickens came back later and her parents found out, she would be in hot water.

"Darned birds," Evelyn groused. She began another circle of the cabin. To the west, well past the coop and the garden, was a pile of small boulders. Her father had put them there when he cleared the ground for their cabin. She moved toward them. Occasionally the chickens strayed that way. The rooster liked to climb on top and crow and gaze out over his domain.

Evelyn walked within a few feet and saw no sign of them and was about to turn when her eye was caught by something lying in the dirt. "No," she said, and dashed over. It was one of the missing chickens, dead. She'd never much cared to touch dead things, so she nudged it with her toe. It was stiff; it had been dead a while. She bent and sought sign of why it died. There were no bites or claw marks as if a predator got at it. But then, a meat-eater wouldn't let it go to waste but would carry it off to feed on.

Evelyn went around the pile. She hadn't taken half a dozen steps when she came on the second chicken. One look at it on its back with its legs sticking out was enough. She nudged it anyway, but life had long since fled.

"What killed them?" Evelyn asked aloud. Bending, she scrunched her mouth in loathing, gripped a leg, and lifted. She would take the chicken back to her pa and let him figure it out. She turned to go and almost at her elbow something moved among the boulders. She looked, and turned to ice.

A thick, sinewy shape had reared. A forked tongue flicked and reptilian eyes regarded her with sinister intensity.

Evelyn fought down fear. The tongue had nearly brushed her arm when it licked out. She didn't dare move, didn't dare do anything that might incite it to bite.

The snake rose higher and its tail buzzed.

Sweat oozed from Evelyn's every pore. Of all God's creatures, to her rattlesnakes were some of the scariest.

The rattler was turning its head from side to side as if it were studying her and couldn't make up its mind what she was.

A drop of sweat trickled down Evelyn's nose onto her upper lip. She considered throwing the chicken at the snake to distract it and then running, and decided not to try. Better that she wait for it to lose interest and crawl off.

The snake went on staring.

Evelyn's whole body was rigid with anxiety. She

felt more drops trickle down. One got into her left eye and stung like the dickens. She resisted an impulse to blink.

From the cabin came a shout; her pa, calling her name.

Evelyn yearned to reply. She yearned to tell him of her peril and have him rush to help. He would shoot it. He was an incredible shot. She once saw him shoot the head off a grouse in flight. He shot the head so the body would be in one piece when her mother served it.

"Evelyn? Where are you?"

Evelyn didn't answer. Everyone claimed that if you stood as still as could be, a snake wouldn't bite. She hoped it was true. Another drop missed her right eye and dribbled onto her cheek.

The rattler was still glaring at her. It didn't make a sound except for the buzzing.

Evelyn swallowed and came to the conclusion she must do something. She couldn't stand there forever. Sooner or later she would involuntarily flinch or twitch.

"Evelyn? Answer me."

Her pa was closer. Evelyn started to turn her head but caught herself. Willpower was called for. Gobs and gobs of willpower. She wasn't like her brother, Zach, who could latch on to things with an intensity that was frightening, or even like her pa who when he concentrated on something devoted his whole will to it. But she was strong-minded and when she put her mind to a purpose she usually did what she set out to do.

"Evelyn? If you can hear me, give a shout."

Oh, that Evelyn could. She watched the snake,

hoping against hope it would slither down into the boulders. But it didn't. It stared and rattled, stared and rattled.

"Evelyn!"

Her father was so close that Evelyn heard his footsteps. She went to whisper but her vocal cords were frozen. All that came out was a low bleat.

"Evelyn?"

Evelyn sensed he was so near she could reach out and touch him. He had to have spotted the snake, even as dark as it had become.

"When I tell you, drop the chicken and leave the rest to me. Do nothing but let go of the chicken. Don't move or yell. Just let it drop. Blink once if you are ready."

Evelyn's whole body broke out in goose bumps. She blinked.

"I'll count to three. On three let go."

The strain was getting to Evelyn. Her legs started to shake. The weight of the chicken seemed to grow tenfold.

"One."

Evelyn swallowed. The rattlesnake hadn't moved, hadn't done a thing when her father spoke, as if it were ignoring him and concentrating solely on her.

"Two."

Evelyn's nerves jangled. She trusted her pa more than anyone, trusted him to do whatever it took, but she was still scared.

"Three."

Evelyn let go. Instantly, the snake struck, biting at the chicken as it fell. Simultaneously, iron hands closed on Evelyn and she was swept away from the boulders as if she were weightless and deposited as gently as a feather on the balls of her feet. It happened so swiftly she had no time to react. Her father released her and she glimpsed a streak of . . . something . . . and heard a sound like metal on rock. The object streaked again and she recognized it; his tomahawk. "Careful," she said, worried the snake might bite him.

Nate grunted and straightened. In his right hand was the tomahawk. In his left was about six inches of rattlesnake, including its head. The mouth opened and closed and went on opening and closing even though most of the body was missing. "You're safe."

"Oh, Pa." Evelyn threw herself at him and hugged him. "Thank goodness you came along when you did."

"I wondered what was keeping you," Nate said, sounding as if he had come down with a cold.

"Another chicken is dead besides that one," Evelyn informed him. "I think maybe the rattler bit them both."

"Another damn rattlesnake," Nate said.

Evelyn rarely heard him swear. A lot of men, and women, too, cussed as if their lives depended on it, but not her father or her mother or her uncle Shakespeare either. She'd asked her father once why he didn't and he said that he never got into the habit. She'd asked Shakespeare, too, and he had chuckled in that merry way he had and said that cussing was for those who "had not so much brains as earwax."

"I have half a mind to call another hunt. I should send you to fetch your brother and your uncle and make plans for tomorrow."

Evelyn's insides churned. She wouldn't get to see Dega and she dearly wanted to. "Is that really necessary?"

"You were nearly bit."

"But I wasn't. And the last hunt didn't turn up many. Another hunt won't either."

"They have to be coming from somewhere," Nate said. "If we can find their den we can put an end to them."

Evelyn thought fast. "It could be anywhere. You could spend a month of Sundays looking and still not find it."

"I suppose."

"And there are the Worths to think of. They're looking forward to their new cabin. Another delay might upset them. Emala, especially. She misses having a home. She told me so, herself. She misses it so much, she was practically in tears over it."

"They have been through a lot," Nate said.

"Then why not just tell everyone about the snake tomorrow and warn them to be on their guard?" Evelyn suggested. "That should do."

Nate looked at the snake's head and scowled and threw it at the pile of boulders. "I am so sick of rattlesnakes. But I reckon you're right. I don't need to be a laughingstock twice in one month."

"No one laughed at you, Pa."

"Your uncle Shakespeare did. He said that if worry was gold I'd be covered in yellow warts."

Evelyn laughed.

"It's too bad a rattler hasn't bitten him."

"Oh, Pa."

Chapter Eleven

The cabin began to take shape.

All the logs were trimmed and cut. Those for the front and the back walls were fourteen feet long; those for the sides, twelve feet. All the notches were a foot from each end. Since the logs weren't the same diameter, Nate and Shakespeare alternated those with slightly thicker ends. That way the walls were even.

Lifting the heavy logs went smoothly until the walls were about chest high. Then they had to resort to skids; smaller logs were braced against each wall, and the cabin logs were rolled up into position. When the walls were head high, they used ropes and the skids.

A fireplace was a necessity. Without it, the Worths would be hard-pressed to survive the bitterly harsh mountain winters. Accordingly, Nate cut slits in one of the upper logs on the wall where the fireplace would go so that when the cabin was done they could insert a saw and make an opening for the fireplace stones.

The roof logs were the longest of all, to allow for an overhang. Getting them up took coordinated effort, and once they were high enough they had to be carefully slid into place. It was a slow process, which was why the roof alone took four days to complete.

Nate and Shakespeare had also left slits in the walls for the door and the window. They cut the door opening down to the ground, and Emala mentioned that she would like it a bit wider.

"May I ask why?" Nate asked.

Emala put her hands on her wide hips and answered, "So I don't get stuck. I'd rather not have to go in and out of my own house sideways."

"I don't blame you, madam," Shakespeare said.

"It is a trial being plump," Emala informed them.

Shakespeare grinned and gave a courtly bow and winked. "But you jiggle so nicely."

"Why, Mr. McNair!" Emala exclaimed, and laughed heartily.

They made the window a foot and a half across, and Emala remarked that she would like it wider, too.

"I don't advise that," Nate said.

"I am a big woman," Emala responded. "I'd like to have a window that all of me can stand in front of."

"The wider it is, the more cold air it will let in," Nate warned her. "Curtains and shutters won't help much when it's cold enough to freeze your breath."

"I hope to get glass like Winona and you have."

"Glass lets in the cold, too. Didn't you notice that our windows are the same size as the windows I am making you?"

Emala reluctantly settled for a small window.

Every day they stopped work at noon to eat and rest. The women cooked food, coffee and tea were brewed, and everyone sat around talking and joking and having a friendly time.

It was during a noon break one day that Randa

got up and strolled off with her hands clasped behind her slender back, admiring the splendid scenery. She loved the sweep of the high mountains. She loved the colors of the vegetation that covered the valley floor. She loved the lake with all the waterfowl cavorting about. In short, she loved everything about their new home.

Randa's ambling brought her to the gully. She was standing watching a bald eagle soar high in the sky when Zach King came out of the trees with his rifle over his shoulder, carrying a rabbit. She remembered him going off earlier and had wondered where he got to. "More food for the pot?" She hadn't heard a shot.

Zach nodded.

Randa had noticed he didn't talk much. He wasn't always gabbing like Chickory did. She liked that. She liked, too, how handsome he was. Not that she would ever let him know, him being married and all. "How is Louisa doin'?"

Zach stopped. "Fine," he said. "She gets a little sick in the mornings, but she is eating like a horse."

Randa grinned and said, "You shouldn't ought to talk about your missus that way."

"It's the truth," Zach said. "I can barely keep enough food in the pantry, she eats so much."

"I hear ladies do that," Randa admitted.

Zach stared at her waist.

"Is somethin' the matter?" Randa asked, uncomfortable under his gaze. "Why are you lookin' at me like that?"

"Where are your weapons?"

"Pardon?"

"You don't even have a knife."

"I do so have one, but I took it off to work," Randa told him.

"No gun?"

"Not yet. My pa says he's fixin' to get me one just as soon as he can afford to," Randa revealed.

"Come over to our cabin later," Zach said. "I have a spare pistol you can have."

"I couldn't." Randa's mother had warned her about accepting gifts even from people she knew and liked.

"I wasn't asking. You can't traipse around out here unarmed, woman. You're asking to be torn to bits or have your throat slit."

Randa felt an odd sort of tingle when he called her "woman." "It can't be as bad as all that."

"It's worse." Zach came closer. "Hasn't my pa or Shakespeare talked to you? Don't be fooled. It's peaceful at the moment, but the peace never lasts. As surely as you're standing there, sooner or later something or someone will try to kill you."

"Happens to you a lot, does it?" Randa teased.

A shadow seemed to pass over Zach's face. "Sometimes it seems as if it happens every time I turn around."

Randa made bold to ask, "My pa says you've killed a lot of folks. Is that true? Are you a killer?"

"It's not anything I like to talk about."

"Oh. Sorry," Randa said quickly, and walked away along the gully rim, intending to go around and into the woods. To her surprise, Zach fell into step beside her.

"Where are you going?"

"Just walkin'."

"I'll go with you. You shouldn't go anywhere unarmed."

"There's really no need," Randa said. "Everyone is

right over yonder. All I need to do is yell and they'll come on the run."

"By the time they got here a bear could rip your head off or tear open your belly."

"You sure think of nice things."

"I think of real things."

Randa puckered her mouth in displeasure. "You're only sayin' that to scare me."

"No, I'm saying it because it's true." Zach touched her arm and she stopped. "Listen to me, Randa, and listen good. If not for your sake then for your family's." He gestured, encompassing the entire valley. "Life here isn't like what you are used to. This isn't like back East. You can't take it for granted that you'll get through the day without something or someone trying to make worm food of you. Always stay alert. Every minute. Every second. The time you don't is the time you die."

Randa still didn't think it could be as bad as he was saying, but she kept her peace. "I'm grateful for the advice."

Zach drew his Bowie and held it so the blade glistened in the sun. "Out here life is like this knife."

"How is that?"

"Beautiful but with a razor's edge. It can take your life as fast as you can blink."

Randa had never thought of a knife as beautiful. "You have a nice way with words."

Frowning, Zach slid the Bowie into its sheath. "If I do, it is news to me. But I hope I've made my point. I'd hate for anything to happen to you."

"You would?"

"Of course. You and your family are our friends. We are—" Zach stopped and his eyes darted toward the gully. "Did you see that?"

"What?" Randa looked but saw only the rocks and boulders that lined the gully's rim.

"I thought I saw a snake." Zach stuck the tail of the dead rabbit under his belt. He leveled his rifle and thumbed back the hammer and went over, stepping carefully.

Randa followed. She was fascinated by him. He had an air. He moved so quick, too. She looked down into the gully but all she saw was more boulders and rocks. "I don't see nothin'."

"Me neither. But I'm sure I did."

"What kind of snake was it?" Randa remembered the fuss everyone was making over rattlers.

"I can't rightly say." Zach shrugged. "Oh well. It's gone now." He let down the hammer and jerked the rabbit from under his belt. "Remember what I've told you. And don't stay out here by yourself." He made for the cabin and the gathering.

Randa lingered, watching him. He sure was forceful. She liked that, too. She idly picked up a small stone and sent it skittering to the bottom of the gully. It clattered noisily when it hit. She went to follow Zach, and stopped. A strange sound had risen. Bending, she tilted her head to hear better. She'd never heard anything like it. It reminded her of the buzzing of a bunch of bees. Near as she could tell it came from the bottom of the gully. She started to go down to investigate.

"Are you coming?"

Randa turned. Zach King had stopped and was waiting for her. She hurried to catch up, saying, "Sorry. I thought I heard something."

"What?"

"I don't know. Maybe bees."

"There are a lot of them hereabouts. Be careful you don't get stung."

"Thank you for lookin' out for me," Randa said quietly. She had never had a man do that except her pa and her brother, but she didn't think of Chickory as a man.

Zach shrugged. "We're an island of people in a sea of savage. We need to watch out for each other."

"Goodness, you really *do* have a way with words," Randa praised him.

"No one has ever said that to me before," Zach said. "If I do, it probably comes from being around Shakespeare so much. His speech is as flowery as a rose garden."

"There you go again."

Zach smiled.

Randa liked his teeth. They were white and even. She liked his eyes, too. They were as green as grass and as deep as the lake. She envied Louisa King. Without thinking she said, "Your wife sure is lucky to have you."

"There are days when she doesn't think so," Zach said. "I tend to aggravate her now and then."

"Doin' what?"

"Being male."

"How is that an aggravation?"

Zach looked at her. "According to her and my mother and Blue Water Woman and just about every married lady I've ever met, it comes naturally. Men can't help but rub women wrong, as my ma likes to say."

"My ma would likely say the same," Randa said. "She's always naggin' my pa about one thing or another. Do this or don't do that and land sakes why can't he ever listen to her."

"There you have it," Zach said.

Randa enjoyed talking to him; he was easy to talk to. She gazed into his eyes and then glanced away. "I hope I meet a fella like you one day. I wouldn't think he was any aggravation at all."

"There's only ever one of us. And you might want someone who doesn't have my flaws."

"What would they be?"

At that juncture Emala came around the cabin and jabbed a thick finger at Randa. "There you are. I've been lookin' all over for you. Where did you get to, youngun?"

"I went for a walk."

"Well, don't go waltzin' off without you lettin' us know. We're not on the plantation anymore. It ain't safe. Am I right, Mr. King, or am I right?"

"It's Zach, and you're absolutely right." Zach held out the dead rabbit. "Would you do me a favor and give this to my mother?"

Emala curled up her thick lips in distaste. "There's blood all over it and half the head is gone."

Zach wiggled the limp body. "Don't tell me you've never handled game?"

"I have, many a time," Emala said. "But I've never liked blood and the butcherin' can be mighty messy." She used her thumb and the first finger of her left hand to take the rabbit by the tail. "It doesn't have lice, does it? Some dead critters crawl with lice."

"No more than any other animal."

Emala beckoned and Randa joined her as she made for a shady spot where the other women were resting. "What were you talkin' to him about?"

"This and that," Randa answered. "Why?"

"I saw how you were smilin' at him. I've never seen you smile at any man that a way. It better not be why I think it is."

"He's nice, is all."

"The Kings are decent folks. They're doin' more for us than anyone ever has and we should be grateful."

"I am."

"Then don't be walkin' alone with Zach King. He's a married man. It's not proper."

"All we did was talk. Don't make more out of it than there was."

"You don't tell me what to do. I tell you. And I'm tellin' you that we must be as nice to the Kings as they've been to us."

"Talkin' ain't nice?"

"Don't sass me, child." Emala scowled. "You're startin' to worry me. You truly are. Until we're settled in and they've accepted us more, you're not to traipse anywhere with Zachary King. You hear me?"

"Accept us more?" Randa repeated.

"We've been with them a good long while, what with crossin' that prairie and comin' up into these mountains. But that ain't the same as bein' neighbors. Neighbors can talk to neighbors anytime."

"How will I know when I can talk to him?"

"I'll tell you." Emala waddled off. "Mind me, you hear?"

Randa frowned. Her mother was always bossing her around. She didn't like it. She didn't like it one bit. Then a thought hit her so hard she was jarred to her marrow; her folks intended to live there the rest of their lives. Which was fine and dandy, but as Zach King had pointed out, there were precious few people around. And all the men save her brother and Dega were spoken for. Though from the way Evelyn and Dega were carrying on, he was spoken for, too.

What was she to do for a man of her own?

Chapter Twelve

The fireplace took some doing.

They inserted the saw into the slits they had cut and sawed until they had the shape. Samuel did most of the sawing. He asked to. It was his cabin and he didn't think it fair or right that Nate and Shakespeare and Zach were doing most of the work.

Nate smiled and handed him the saw.

While this was going on, the women and the Nansusequas and Chickory went off to gather stones to use in the construction. Evelyn and Dega went one way, Waku and his wife and daughters another, Winona and Blue Water Woman and Emala and Randa yet another.

That left Chickory. He didn't want to go with the women. He especially didn't want to go with his mother. He loved her dearly, but she was always telling him what to do and then complaining that he didn't do it right. He didn't know the Indians well enough to feel comfortable going with them, and he sensed that Evelyn and Dega wanted to be by themselves. That was fine with him. He went off alone, northwest past the gully and into the trees.

A few days ago he had done some exploring and came across a low hill covered with stones that might do.

Chickory hummed as he walked. He kept his hand on the hilt of the knife Shakespeare McNair had given him. Now there was a strange person, he reflected. Half the time, he had no idea whatsoever what that white man was talking about. It was all that Bard stuff. Chickory had never heard of the Bard of Avon; he didn't even know what a Bard was. Or an Avon, for that matter.

It had surprised him, the old man giving him the knife. He'd never imagined white folks could be like Shakespeare and Nate King. The whites back at the plantation had either bossed him around or looked down their noses at him. It was . . . Chickory thought hard for the right word . . . it was *refreshing* to meet white people who treated him as if his skin color didn't matter.

Chickory looked down at himself. His skin might not matter but his size sure did. He was too skinny. All lean muscle and bone. His pa said that he would fill out as he grew, but that could take a while. Chickory wished he would fill out now. He wanted to be big and strong, like his father.

It didn't help that he had lost a lot of weight when he came down sick at Bent's Fort. No one could figure out why. One of the men who ran the trading post, Ceran St. Vrain, had pestered him with questions. Had he drank any stagnant water? That was the word St. Vrain used: "stagnant." Chickory had to ask what it meant and St. Vrain said it meant water that had been standing a long time and maybe smelled funny or was brown or some other unusual color. Had he been stung by mosquitoes? St. Vrain wanted to know. Land sakes, Chickory had been stung by an army of them. Had he been bit by any spiders? Chickory remembered one he found in his blankets when he woke up, but he didn't recall it biting him unless the spider bit him in his sleep.

The crack of a twig brought Chickory out of himself. He stopped and tightened his hand on the knife. If there was one thing he'd learned about the wilds, it was to be cautious. There were bears and those big cats to watch out for, and Nate King had said there were buffalo in the mountains, too, although not nearly as many as down on the prairie.

The brush rustled and out stepped a doe. She was young and small and took short, timid steps, her ears pricked, her nostrils quivering. She had caught his scent but was unsure where he was.

Chickory grinned. He flapped his arms and said, "Boo!"

The doe's tail shot up and she fled in great bounding leaps, her legs tucked together. Within moments the vegetation swallowed her.

Chuckling, Chickory walked on. He liked the woods, although they sure were spooky. He hadn't said anything to anyone, but he was particularly scared of being eaten. He kept having dreams, or rather, nightmares, in which a bear or one of those cats or once a critter McNair had called a wolverine, caught him and ate him. In his nightmares he always screamed and tried to get away as their teeth and their claws bit into him. One night he woke up in a cold sweat, afraid he had cried out in his sleep, but the rest of his family slept blissfully on.

Chickory swallowed the memory. No, sir. Being eaten wasn't a good way to die. Although, now that he thought about it, he couldn't think of a way that was good. He liked being alive. The world was a wonderful place, and there was a lot of it he had yet to explore. His folks seemed to take it for granted he would live there the rest of his days, but he had other ideas. In a few years he was going to leave the mountains and do some traveling. Maybe he would come back, and maybe he wouldn't.

Chickory hadn't told his parents. His pa would likely understand, but his ma would blubber.

Presently the pines and spruce and the oaks thinned, and Chickory came out into an open area near the bottom of the hill. Above him flat rocks and jumbled stones were dotted by a few boulders.

Large round stones, Nate King had said, so that's what Chickory looked for. He started up and glimpsed movement. Something had darted under a rock.

A lizard, maybe, Chickory thought, or possibly one of those chipmunks. It wasn't long enough to be a snake. He found a rock he reckoned would be suitable and carried it down and deposited it at the bottom and went back up for another. They were heavy, and after half a dozen he stopped and ran his forearm across his sweaty forehead.

In the trees a pair of birds flitted from branch to branch. One was yellow and the other a dull gray. They alighted and the yellow one broke into marvelous song. Chickory wondered if they might be finches. He wasn't good with bird names, but there had been finches back at the plantation and these reminded him of a lot of them.

Chickory went on gathering rocks. He would need help getting them all back. He bent and tried to lift one but it was firm in the ground. Prying with his fingertips, he got his fingers underneath, and pulled. The rock rose an inch. Gritting his teeth and flexing, Chickory tried again. This time the rock came off the ground. He raised it to his knees, and stopped.

From under it crawled a snake.

Chickory didn't understand how a snake could have been under there, as embedded as the rock was. He went to straighten and his breath caught in his throat. The triangle of its head, the pattern of its skin, the segments at the end of the tail—it was a rattlesnake. No sooner did he realize it than the snake coiled and raised baleful eyes in his direction.

Chickory stared back. His ma had told him that the Lord had set mankind over the beasts and that nine times out of ten a person could set a beast to running off just by looking at it.

This must be the tenth time. The rattler stayed where it was.

Chickory didn't want to get bit. He stood still, his arms starting to hurt from the strain of the heavy rock. The snake went on staring. Its eyes were scary. They weren't like the eyes of anything Chickory knew. He didn't like how its tongue kept flicking out at him either. And what a tongue, forked as it was.

Chickory swallowed. He couldn't hold the rock forever.

The snake stopped rattling. It lowered its head and slowly turned and began to crawl off.

Chickory raised the rock higher—and threw it at the snake. He jumped back as he did, and whooped with glee when the rock thudded down right on the reptile. The head and some of the body poked out from under and it began to hiss and twist and turn. Chickory picked up another big rock and dropped it on top of the flat one.

The rattlesnake went limp.

"Got you, did I?" Chickory gloated. "That's what you get for spookin' me." He kicked at the rocks, but the snake didn't move. Careful as could be, he slid the rock off. Most of the snake was crushed pulp.

Chickory laughed and smacked his thigh. "I done did it. Killed me a rattlesnake. All by myself."

Chickory hadn't had to kill much growing up on the plantation. A few frogs and birds and snakes and that was it.

When his family and the Kings were crossing the prairie his pa had let him shoot game a few times. He would have gotten more, except deer and the like were hard to find and he wasn't the world's best shot. Fact was, he was lucky to hit the broadside of a tree from twenty steps away. But he was getting better. Give him time, Nate King had said, and he'd be able to drop a deer at a hundred yards.

Chickory couldn't wait.

Deep in thought, Chickory carried the gore-spattered rock to his growing pile and was about to set it down when he changed his mind and cast it aside. His mother wouldn't want no gory rocks in her fireplace. He went back up the hill. Again he thought he saw something dart away.

Chickory came to a hump and couldn't believe his eyes. Above him were enough flat rocks to make half the fireplace—and rattlesnakes were coiled on a good many of them, sunning themselves. None rose up in alarm or hissed or rattled. Maybe they didn't realize he was there. He began counting and stopped at eleven. He'd never seen so many rattlers in one place at one time. There were big ones and not so big. All were ugly as sin. It gave him nervous twinges to look at them.

He was lucky he had spotted them. If he hadn't, he'd have blundered into a nest of fangs and been bit so many times, he'd have been dead before he could turn around.

The smart thing was to get out of there, but Chickory stayed. He was fascinated. Here was another part of why he liked the wilderness so much.

There was always something new, something unexpected, like those buffalo on the plains and that raccoon they caught in their camp and the black bear that came sniffing around one night.

A rattler stirred. Its head rose a few inches and it looked around and then twisted and crawled off the flat rock toward another flat rock that already had a snake on it.

Chickory thought they would fight. He watched in breathless wonder as the first snake reached the second snake and crawled up over it and lay with their bodies touching. That was all. No hissing or rattling or biting or nothing.

"He your friend?" Chickory said out loud.

Another snake near to him raised its head and the tip of its tail moved, rattling lightly.

Chickory put his hand on his knife. The rattlesnake was flicking its tongue but it didn't bare its fangs or come toward him. After a bit it lost interest and sank back down, coiling so its head was under its body.

Chickory had seen enough. He backed away, glancing behind him and to either side, alert for more serpents.

On the way down he picked up three flat rocks. It was as many as he could carry.

He started for the cabin site.

"I should tell Pa about the snakes," Chickory said to himself, then shook his head. If he told his pa, his pa would tell his mother, and his mother would forbid him to ever come anywhere near that hill for as long as he drew breath. She was always doing stuff like that, always spoiling his fun. He decided to keep it a secret. He wouldn't say a word so he could come back whenever he wanted and watch the snakes. He didn't consider them much of a threat. They were far from the cabins.

He did wonder where they all came from.

The gully appeared. Chickory hadn't been down in it, but he planned to go once the cabin was done. He had a lot of exploring to do. The valley was filled with animals and sights worth seeing.

Chickory gazed over his shoulder at a high mountain with a block of white at the top. A glacier, it was called. Shakespeare McNair had told him about it, said it was made all of ice and never melted. Claimed, too, that the Worths should stay away from up there, that it was slippery and covered with cracks that once a person fell in, they never got out. McNair also said that now and then he and his wife and the Kings heard strange roars and howls from some sort of creature. That was what McNair called it: a creature. Not an animal. It sounded like another of McNair's tall tales to Chickory.

Randa was carrying rocks, too. She set hers down and waited as he brought his over.

"Those are good ones. Where did you get them?"

"Off a ways," Chickory said, with a jerk of his thumb.

"Are there more? I'll go with you and bring some back."

"There aren't any more."

"You're lyin'," Randa said.

If there was one thing Chickory hated it was to be called a liar—even when he was lying. "What makes you say that?"

"I know you. I know how you talk when you lie. Why won't you tell me where you got them?"

Chickory hesitated. He would love to tell someone and his sister was pretty good at keeping a secret. "If I do, you have to give me your word you won't say a word to anybody."

"You have it," Randa said.

Chickory gave his account, ending with, "That hill is crawlin' with them. You want to come, you have to be careful."

"You need to go tell Mr. King."

"No. Ma will find out, and you know what she'll do."

"You have to," Randa insisted. "Remember that hunt? This could be what Mr. King was lookin' for." She pointed. "There he is right there. Go over and tell him or I'll do it myself."

Chickory bit off a sharp reply. He was mad. He'd trusted her and she'd betrayed him. Now he wouldn't get to go watch the snakes whenever he wanted.

"Do it. Now."

"Just because you are older than me . . ." Chickory wheeled and walked over to where Nate King and Shakespeare McNair were working on the fireplace. "I brought some rocks," he announced.

Without looking up Nate said, "We need a lot. Keep looking."

"Yes, sir." Chickory stayed where he was.

"Anything else?" McNair asked.

"I just want to thank you both for bein' so kind to us, and all. If there is ever somethin' I can do for you, let me know."

Nate raised his head and chuckled. "You can find more rocks."

Chickory nodded and walked back to his sister.

"There. I told him. He said he'd go have a look later, after he's done with the cabin."

"You did the right thing," Randa said. "I'm proud of you."

Chapter Thirteen

The fireplace took four days to build. It took so long because they had to bring the clay they used for the mortar from a quarter of a mile away.

The men did the digging and piled the clay on a travois; Winona and Blue Water Woman took turns riding the horse that pulled it. They mixed the clay with water and dirt and laid the stones and once the mix dried it was as hard as the stones themselves.

The front door posed a problem. They had no boards or planks. They didn't have a sawmill to make them either. The alternatives were to split logs and spend tedious hours planing and smoothing or go all the way to Bent's Fort. Shakespeare struck on a temporary solution. They would get boards at Bent's on their regular supply trek. In the meantime, the Worths had to make do with Shakespeare's bedroom door. He took it off its hinges and brought it over and hung it himself. While it was wide enough it wasn't quite long enough; there was a gap of two inches at the top. When Emala asked why Shakespeare didn't leave the gap at the bottom, he smiled and said, "So every bug in creation can crawl inside and make itself at home?"

"Lordy, no, I wouldn't like that," Emala agreed. "A gap at the top is fine by me."

"We can't thank you enough for the use of your door," Samuel said.

"When we go to Bent's we'll have a door made

that will fit proper," Shakespeare promised. "That should be in three weeks or so."

Samuel patted the wall and beamed. "Our new home," he said proudly. "Our very own by-God new home."

"Don't take the Lord's name in vain," Emala said. "He saw us safe all the way here. The least you can do is show respect."

"I am as thankful as I can be," Samuel replied. He turned to Shakespeare and shook his hand and then to Nate and shook his. "I don't have the words to say how much this means."

"What are friends for?" Nate said.

"That's just it," Samuel said, and looked away and coughed. "I ain't never had friends like you two. Not in all my born days."

Shakespeare launched into a quote. "I do profess to be no less than I seem; to serve him truly that will put me in trust; to love him that is honest; to converse with him that is wise and says little; to fear judgment; to fight when I cannot chose, and to eat no fish."

"He's saying he was happy to be of service," Nate translated.

"What was that about fish?" Emala asked. "Don't you ever eat it?"

"Personally I like fish now and then so long as it doesn't taste too fishy."

"How can fish not taste like fish?"

"You have to excuse him," Nate said. "He often has no idea what he is talking about."

Shakespeare snorted.

"May I tell you two gentlemen something?" Samuel said earnestly. "There are times when I have no notion of what you are talkin' about."

Winona and Blue Water Woman joined them, and Winona said, "Guess what, husband?"

"You want to take me home and ravish me."

Emala squealed in delight and exclaimed, "Mr. King! The things that come out of your mouth. You are a caution."

"He thinks he is," Winona said. "But no, that is not it. We have decided to have a . . . what do you whites call it?" She puckered her brow. "Now I remember. A housewarming. All of us will bring food tomorrow afternoon to celebrate building the new cabin and to welcome the Worths to our valley. How does that sound?"

"I have ale I'll bring," Shakespeare offered.

"So long as you don't drink too much," Blue Water Woman said. "Remember how you become when you have had more than one."

"Remind me."

"You become frisky."

"Me?"

"Very frisky."

Emala squealed once more. "I swear. You folks talk as if you just fell in love."

Shakespeare clasped Blue Water Woman's hand and sank to one knee. "But soft, what light through yonder window breaks? It is the east, and Juliet is the sun. Arise, fair sun, and kill the envious moon, who is already sick and pale with grief, that thou, her maid, art far more fair than she."

"Do you see what I must put up with?" Blue Water Woman said.

"O speak again, bright angel!"

"I think he's adorable," Emala gushed.

Blue Water Woman patted the top of McNair's

head. "You do not have to live with him day in and day out."

"Ouch," Shakespeare said.

Nate chuckled and walked toward the lake. Halfway there he acquired a shapely shadow.

"Leaving without your horse?" Winona asked.

Nate held up his encrusted hands. "I need to wash up and then we can go."

"Any regrets about inviting the Worths to our valley?"

"Why would you ask a thing like that? They're good people. They'll make good neighbors."

"I remember you saying once that this valley was ours and ours alone. Yet you allowed the Nansusequas to stay and now you have allowed the Worths to move here, too." Winona rose onto the tips of her toes and kissed him on his chin. "You would make a fine *sosoni*."

"I thought I already was. Your people adopted me into the tribe years ago."

"I stand corrected," Winona said, taking his arm. "You are right, though. They are good people. I hope the next family will be just as good."

"Next?" Nate said, and stopped. "Whoa there, silly goose. The Worths are the last. There will be no more after them." He'd never intended for anyone other than his family and Shakespeare and Blue Water Woman to settle there. It was to be their haven, their sanctuary, so far into the mountains that they would never be intruded upon.

"So you say," Winona teased.

"Straight tongue," Nate said. "From here on out, no one comes through that pass without my say-so."

"What will you do? Put up a sign?"

Nate hadn't thought of that but now that he did,

he said, "I'll have one up by the end of the week. A warning to trespassers to keep out, that this valley is spoken for."

"It is a big valley."

Indeed it was. Nate scanned the sun-washed lofty mountains, the ranks of emerald forest, the expanse of blue lake dotted by meandering waterfowl. "A hundred homesteaders could live here comfortably."

"But you will not let them."

"I will not."

"I don't know, husband," Winona said uncertainly. "I foresee trouble for us down the road, as you whites would say."

"We'll cross that bridge when we come to it, as us whites would say," Nate retorted. Sliding his arms around her waist, he kissed her on the forehead. "We have a right to protect our own and this valley is ours. We found it. We claimed it. We settled it. If I could, I would register our claim with the government so that it was legal, but I can't because there *is* no government. Out here it's every man, or woman, for him- or herself."

"White ways have long puzzled me," Winona confessed. "Your people think of land differently from my people. We do not own it in the way whites like to. In our eyes the land is for everyone to use."

"Not to whites and not this valley," Nate stressed. "I grant you we look at it differently. But I can't let folks come waltzing in here as they please or pretty soon we'll have a whole settlement and be up to our armpits in people and rules and laws and I won't have that. Civilization ends at the Mississippi River. I, for one, am glad it does."

Winona nodded. She had heard all this before.

"How far are you willing to go to keep this valley ours?"

"As far as I need to."

"You would kill to keep people out?"

Nate shrugged. "Like I said, dear heart, we'll cross that bridge when we come to it."

"You are being evasive."

"I'm being honest. No, I don't want to kill. But I will keep this valley ours no matter what it takes."

"There is much more wilderness, you know," Winona mentioned. "Many thousands of your miles. Enough for everyone."

Nate placed his chin on the top of her head and gazed at a pair of geese out on the lake. "I wish you were right. But you don't know my people like I do. They are never happy with what they have. They always have to have more. They've pushed from the Atlantic to the Mississippi and have so overrun the land that it won't be long before they push past it. It will be like a dam bursting. Whites will spill across the prairie and into these mountains until there will barely be breathing space."

"You exaggerate, surely."

Nate drew back and looked into her eyes. "I wish I did. I wish I could make you see. Trust me on this. A time will come, maybe in our lifetimes, when my people will want all this land for their own."

"And what of my people? What of the other tribes?"

"My people will do to them as they did to the tribes back East. They'll exterminate them or make them live where the tribes do not want to live."

Winona did not hide how troubled she was. "You have rarely been wrong about anything, but I hope you are wrong about this. For if what you say is true, blood will be spilled."

"There will be blood," Nate agreed. He hugged her close and she clasped him tighter and they stood a while with the sun warm on their faces and the breeze in their hair and a robin warbling in the woods.

That night Nate lay on his back in their bed with Winona's cheek on his chest and was unable to get to sleep. He was troubled by their talk. He had a feeling, a sense he could not account for, of trouble looming on their horizon. He tried to blame it on nerves, but he knew better. Life was what it was, at times peaceful and wonderful and at times violent and savage. They could ward off the ugly aspects but they couldn't hold those aspects at bay indefinitely. Life wouldn't let them. When people least expected, life slammed them to the ground and ripped at them with claws of strife and misery.

There was a passage in the Bible that Nate had always liked, about how God sent his rain on the just and the unjust. Which was as it should be, Nate supposed, but not much comfort to those being rained on. Because it wasn't just rain. It was death and disease and hurt and slaughter and the many sorrows the human soul had to endure.

Nate stared at the ceiling. If he lived to be a hundred, he doubted he would savvy why people had to suffer. The best he could do was protect his family so they suffered as little as possible.

With that in mind, he dozed off.

The next morning dawned clear. The lake was a brilliant blue in a world of lush green. Nate dipped their bucket in to fill it and saw fish swim by. When he got back to the cabin Winona was busy making food for the get-together.

Everyone had agreed to meet at the Worth cabin shortly after the sun was at its zenith. The food would be set out, and they would talk and play games and have fun until late into the night. Nate was looking forward to it. So when he stepped outside shortly before noon and saw the western sky, he scowled.

A dark cloud bank blotted out the horizon, a thunderhead rent by flashes of lightning. As yet it was too distant to hear the thunder. But in a while it would be upon them. He went back in and informed his wife.

"I hope it passes over quickly," Winona said.

So did Nate. Otherwise it would spoil their plans. He went back out and made sure the corral gate was secure and brought in all his tools so they wouldn't get wet and rust. As he was carrying his ax in he heard the first far-off rumble and smelled moisture in the air. It wouldn't be long.

The first drops were big and cold. They hit like gunshots on the roof. The wind picked up and churned the surface of the lake with wavelets. Lightning crashed and thunder boomed, and the dark sky opened up and unleashed a deluge. The rain fell in sheets. It was so heavy that Nate, standing at his window, couldn't see the chicken coop or the woodshed only a dozen yards out.

Winona came to his side and peered into the torrent. "Please do not last long," she said to the heavens.

A cannonade of thunder shook their cabin. Evelyn came out of her room and took one look and said, "This better not keep me from seeing Dega."

"Oh?" Nate said.

Evelyn blushed.

The storm lasted more than an hour. It rained so

hard that at its peak the ground was inches deep in water. Gradually the downpour tapered to a sprinkle and ended entirely. The sky turned from black to gray and then to blue. In its wake it left pools and puddles and mud and muck.

Nate was still at the window, Winona at the counter placing a pie she had baked in a basket. "It's a mess out there," he said. "I should go tell everyone to hold off a couple of hours. Give things time to dry out."

Evelyn jumped up from a chair by the table. "Let me, Pa. I'm tired of being cooped up."

"Is that the only reason?"

Evelyn blushed again. "Of course."

"You'll have to ride careful. The ground is slippery."

"I will. Don't worry," Evelyn said. "Nothing will happen."

Chapter Fourteen

During the height of the storm the rain cascaded into the gulley as water over a waterfall. The gully quickly filled. It often did when rain was heavy. Usually it rose to a gap near the bottom and was channeled out and over the adjacent ground before the bottom was covered. This time the rain came down so hard and so fast that the level rose more swiftly than it ever had, and the gap wasn't wide enough for the water to drain out before it covered the gully from end to end.

The rain kept on falling and the level kept on rising and the water reached the cleft and flowed in and down. It poured into the underground chamber like water down a funnel. It drenched the enormous mass of serpents and the mass writhed to life, annoyed. Like strands of unraveling thread, the multitude uncoiled and unwound and swarmed up the cleft. Not by scores or by hundreds but by the thousands. So many filled the cleft that they temporarily stopped the water. In a living torrent of their own they flowed out of the cleft and up and out of the gully onto the ground above. They didn't stop there. The battering rain, the wet and the cold, were not to their liking. In sinuous clusters they fanned out, crawling every which way, anxious in their instinct to escape the wet.

But there was no escape. The rain was so heavy that the ground couldn't absorb it all. The snakes crawled in water inches deep, and they didn't like that. Some crawled faster and farther than they had ever gone, to all points of the compass. Those that fled to the west vanished into the trees. The rest spread out along the lakeshore, living currents of reptilian flesh.

The rain went on and on and the snakes crawled and crawled until finally the black clouds drifted east, the lightning and thunder dwindled and the rain became a mist that soon ended.

In many places the water was still inches deep, with scattered pools and countless puddles.

Nearly everywhere, the water moved as if alive.

Evelyn King couldn't saddle her horse fast enough. She was eager to be on her errand. She would give her father's message to the Worths and her brother and his wife and then ride on to the Nansusequa lodge and give the message to them, and get to see Dega.

As Evelyn smoothed the saddle blanket she thought of the night before when she snuck out to see him. A warm tingle spread through her tummy. His kisses were like sweet honey. Strange that a girl would think that of a boy, but there it was.

Evelyn swung her saddle on and bent to the cinch. She had chosen a sorrel she was fond of. It had a gentle disposition and never gave her a lick of trouble. The bridle was already on so when she lowered the stirrup all she had to do was swing up and jab her heels and she was away. She was wearing a light blue dress she had made herself and shoes she bought in St. Louis. The shoes were a bit too tight, but they were the fanciest she owned and she wanted to look especially pretty for the get-together, and for Dega.

The thought of him made her warm again. She stayed close to the water's edge where there were fewer rocks and she could go faster. The Worth cabin was off to the northwest a ways and she would have to cross the shore to reach it. Then on to Zach's.

"Why go to them first?" Evelyn asked out loud. She had a better idea. Why not go see Dega first and give the others the news on her way back? The sooner she saw him, the sooner they could sneak off into the woods to hug and kiss. Laughing at her brainstorm, she brought the sorrel to a trot. Its heavy hooves dug deep into the rain-softened earth, leaving broad pockmarks.

To her right was the lake, to her left puddles and pools and areas where the water appeared to be ankle high. She thought she saw something move in one of the puddles.

Evelyn passed the Worths' cabin and her brother's place. Smoke curled from his chimney. The door was closed and the curtains were over the window. She almost hollered a greeting but didn't. If they came out, she would be obligated to stop and she didn't want to stop until she reached the east end of the lake, and Dega.

"You handsome devil," Evelyn said softly. She had never felt about anyone as she did about him.

The sorrel had not been ridden in a while and was eager for the exercise. Head straight, mane flying, it raced along the open belt that edged the lake.

Evelyn glanced at a tract of water-covered ground and noticed dozens of ripples. Odd, she thought, since the wind had nearly died. Almost as if fish were in the water, swimming about. They must be small fish, she reasoned, since the water wasn't very deep. She couldn't account for how they got there since the lake hadn't risen much during the storm. Not like the time a while back when it poured rain for half a day and the lake rose midway to the trees.

Ahead, the belt of clear space narrowed; a strip of rocks and small boulders came down nearly to the water. She slowed and saw that a shallow pool had formed on the near side of the strip. She must cross a swatch of water maybe ten feet wide.

Suddenly the sorrel stopped.

"What on earth?" Evelyn was perplexed. She hadn't pulled on the reins. The horse had halted on its own and now it was staring at the pool.

"What's gotten into you?" Evelyn poked with her heels, but the sorrel just stood there. She didn't know what to make of it. The sorrel had never acted this way. She jabbed her heels harder, but all the sorrel did was bob its head. Annoyed at the delay, she slapped her legs and lashed the reins. The sorrel took a few steps—and stopped.

"You're being contrary," Evelyn complained. She lashed the reins again, but the sorrel wouldn't move. She stared at the water and noticed the same eddies as elsewhere. Could they be minnows? she wondered. Or maybe frogs? She remembered once after a heavy spring rain seeing a lot of frogs.

Evelyn tried yet again to coax the sorrel forward. "Come on, boy. I want to see Dega."

The sorrel bobbed its head and nickered.

Evelyn was losing her patience. There was only one explanation. Some horses didn't like water. She'd never had cause to think the sorrel was one, but that must be the case. She smacked him and whipped him with the reins and he walked into the pool and once again stopped.

Evelyn felt a shaking sensation. With a start, she

realized the sorrel was trembling as if cold or afraid. When it turned its head toward the forest, she turned hers. She figured it must have caught the scent of a bear or a mountain lion. But when she followed the direction of its gaze it hit her that the sorrel wasn't interested in the woodland; it was staring at the pool.

"You're not afraid of a few fish, are you?" Since force hadn't worked, Evelyn resorted to kindness. Bending, she patted the sorrel's neck and spoke soothingly. "There, there. Come on, big fella. You're a good horse. Move those legs of yours. You're keeping me from my man."

The sorrel trembled.

"This is plain stupid," Evelyn declared. She slapped her legs once, twice, three times, and the sorrel edged ahead as if it were walking through brambles. She was pleased, but she was also mad that it was moving so slowly. "I don't have all day."

To her dismay the sorrel once again stopped.

Evelyn glanced down. The water was above the sorrel's hooves. Everywhere there were the strange eddies. Again she tried to get the sorrel to move, but it refused. She was mad and confused. She went to slap her legs as hard as she could and happened to glance down just as the head of a snake rose out of the water near the sorrel's front leg and swam past.

Evelyn gasped. She recognized what kind it was; a rattlesnake. Scarcely breathing, she leaned down as far as she dared while clinging to the saddle and peered intently at the movement in the water. Her eyes were slow to adjust to the blend of light and shadow but when they did, fear spiked through her. Those weren't fish. Those weren't frogs. They were snakes. Lots and lots of snakes. And God help her—as near as Evelyn could tell, they were all rattle-snakes.

Evelyn straightened and sat perfectly still. No wonder the sorrel didn't want to move. The horse somehow knew. She looked down, wondering what she should do. The sorrel was only a little way into the water. If she could reach the clear strip that fringed the lake, they would be all right. But which way should she go? Forward or back?

Evelyn's mouth was dry. So many rattlesnakes, so many fangs, so much venom. Should the sorrel and she go down, they would be bitten to death within moments.

"Oh God."

Shifting, Evelyn stared at her brother's cabin. Maybe if she yelled he would hear and come to her aid. She opened her mouth but closed it again. Knowing Zach, he would come charging across the shore, through a dozen pools left by the rain, pools teeming with eddies and the serpents that made them.

"God," Evelyn said again. "What do I do?" She gazed longingly to the east where the Nansusequa lodge was partly visible in the shadow of the big trees. "Dega," she said.

The sorrel gave a hard shake.

Evelyn looked down and her tongue clove to the roof of her mouth. A large rattler was coiled around the sorrel's front leg and was slowly winding up it. She gripped the reins with both hands. She had forgotten her rifle and was glad she had. She could predict what would happen next, and it did.

The sorrel whinnied and exploded into motion. It reared, kicking out with its front legs, seeking to kick off the rattler. The snake slid partway down. Uttering another whinny, the sorrel burst into motion.

It was clear of the water in a few bounds and on the clear strip, but it didn't stay there. It veered away from the lake toward the woods—and toward another, larger, pool.

Evelyn clung on for dear life. She tried to turn but the horse was in a panic. The rattler had fallen off its leg. She wondered if the sorrel had been bitten and prayed not. In front of them loomed the pool. She hauled on the reins with all her might but it had no effect. The sorrel galloped headlong into the pool. Water—and snakes—went flying. The water rose fully a foot, hardly enough to deter a full-grown horse. Beyond the pool was a short stretch of open ground. Evelyn had hopes the sorrel would make it if it kept moving fast enough.

Without any warning, the sorrel stopped in the middle of the pool.

"What are you doing?" Evelyn slapped her legs. The water around them was alive.

The sorrel snorted and wouldn't budge.

"Please," Evelyn said, and slapped again. She might as well be trying to get a log to move.

All the sorrel did was shake.

Evelyn didn't blame it. Her skin was crawling. She saw a triangular head break the surface and swim toward them and dip from sight. She couldn't begin to imagine how many snakes there must be.

A pebble's toss away the biggest head yet broke the surface. It rose a good foot and the forked tongue flicked at them and went on flicking as the rattlesnake approached.

The sorrel saw the snake. Its eyes were mirrors of fear. It shook so violently that Evelyn gripped its mane.

The rattlesnake glided closer. It made no sound other than the soft, wet swish of its body cleaving the water.

Evelyn drew one of her pistols. She pointed the heavy flintlock with both hands and thumbed back the hammer. She was nowhere near as good a shot as her brother or her pa or even her ma, but the snake was near enough that she was confident she could hit it. She took a deep breath and held the air in as her father had taught her and aimed at the blunt head and held the pistol as steady as she could. The snake wasn't more than an arm's length from the sorrel. "Please let me hit it," Evelyn said, and fired.

The flintlock belched smoke and lead. To her delight her aim was true. The ball struck the rattler in the head and the head blew apart like a small melon, spattering skin and flesh. The body went into a paroxysm of convulsions.

And the sorrel bolted.

Evelyn had no inkling of what it was about to do. One instant it was motionless, the next it was hurtling pell-mell toward the trees. Instinctively, she grabbed at the reins and the mane. To grip them she had to let go of the flintlock and it fell with a splash.

The sorrel broke out of the pool onto the wet ground.

Holding fast, Evelyn looked down—and almost swooned. Rattlesnakes were wrapped around both front legs and one of the back legs. She saw heads whip and fangs sink in. A terrible certainty gripped her.

The horse veered and another pool barred their way. Without slowing, the sorrel barreled into it. It proved to be the deepest pool yet; the water rose as high as the sorrel's belly. It roiled, and not from the sorrel. Rattlesnakes were everywhere, writhing and twisting. Many attacked the intruder.

Evelyn couldn't help herself. She screamed.

The sorrel slowed. It staggered. Head low, it lurched toward solid ground.

"You can do it," Evelyn coaxed. "Just a little farther." She glanced at the Nansusequa lodge, so distant it might as well be on the moon. "Oh, Dega," she said.

The sorrel stumbled.

A rattlesnake arced at Evelyn's left leg, and she jerked her leg clear. The snake missed and fell back. All she could do was hold on and pray as the sorrel grew weaker and weaker.

The last few feet, the horse could barely stand. Evelyn exhaled in relief when it was clear of the water and kicked to get it to trot. Instead, the sorrel gave a last whinny and pitched onto its side.

Evelyn tried to push clear, but she wasn't fast enough. She uttered a cry of her own as the sorrel crashed down. For a few seconds she lay paralyzed with pain and fright. Then she turned her head toward the pool.

A rattler was slithering toward her.

Chapter Fifteen

Emala Worth felt as snug as a bedbug in a blanket. Although she abhorred bed bugs, just like she did most every other bug. To her way of thinking bugs made no sense. They bit people and crawled on people and got into food. She couldn't for the life of her understand how they fit into the Almighty's scheme of things, but since he had made them, they must have a purpose.

Surprised at her near-blasphemous thought, Emala rolled onto her side to stare at the window.

The rain had finally stopped, the storm finally ended. For a while there, when the elements were fiercely battering their cabin, Emala had been half afraid it would buckle from the ferocity of the storm. But the walls and ceiling held, and with the door shut and a blanket over the window, not much rain got in. It had puddled some under the window, but that was all.

Everyone was resting. Samuel was on the blanket beside her. Randa was on another over by the wall and Chickory was stretched out near the door. Emala looked at each of her children and her heart was filled to overflowing with her love for them. They were everything to her.

Her new home counted for a lot, too. Emala loved the cabin. It was much more spacious than their shack on the plantation. A lot sturdier, too. She couldn't wait for Samuel to build some furniture; a

table and chairs for the family to sit and eat, and a
rocking chair for her, and a bed. Three beds, actually,
since Randa and Chickory were too old to sleep together.

A good wide bed for Samuel and her. She tingled
at the prospect. Next to singing and eating, one of
the things she liked most was nighttime. Nothing
beat that wonderful feeling of being snuggled, warm
and cozy.

Emala closed her eyes. She wanted to rest a bit
more. But everyone would be there soon to eat and
have fun and she had to get up and see that the dirt
floor was smooth and tidy.

That was another thing. They needed a wood
floor. She would speak to Samuel about it just as
soon as he stopped snoring. She marveled that he
had slept through the storm. That man could sleep
through anything.

Over by the door, Chickory Worth was feeling rest-
less. He'd wanted to stand at the window and watch
the rain and the lightning, but his ma made him lie
down and try to get some sleep like they were doing. He heard his mother moving, and then a sound
pierced the stillness. He sat up. "Did you hear that?"

"The thunder far off?" Emala said.

"No. It was a shot." Chickory stood. "I'm sure it
was a shot."

"Maybe Mr. King or Mr. McNair shot somethin'
to eat," Emala said. "I hope it was one of them elks. I
am growin' powerful fond of elk meat."

Chickory stepped to the window and moved the
blanket. The sky was clearing, the gray giving way to
blue. The air smelled fresh, and was on the chill side.
He shivered slightly.

Water covered much of the ground up to several inches deep and appeared to be deeper off toward the gully. Chickory reckoned it would all soon drain away. As he stared, the water rippled as if moved by the wind but he couldn't feel a breeze. "I want to go out and look around, Ma."

"Whatever for? You'll track mud into our new house."

"I'll wipe my feet before I come in."

Emala sighed. The boy always had an answer. "You don't go far, you hear? The Kings and everybody will be here soon and I want you inside when they come."

"Thanks, Ma," Chickory said. He went to the door and opened it and took several steps, the water rising around his bare feet and his ankles. Something rubbed over his toes and he looked down.

The water was filled with snakes.

Louisa lay in bed with her hands on her belly. Zach had insisted she rest before the social and gave her what she liked to call his manly stare. He always got this intense look about him whenever he wanted her to do something for her own good. If she objected, he would argue and today she didn't want to argue.

The patter of the rain on their roof had ceased and the howl of the wind had faded. Silence reigned, save for the ticking of their clock on the mantle above the fireplace. She liked to listen to the soft, regular *tick-tick-tick*. It was so soothing it often put her to sleep.

Lou eased onto her back. Zach wasn't beside her; he had been when she'd lain down. She swung her legs over the side and went out into the main room and there he was, at their table, his legs over it, reading. It startled her. Zach rarely read. He wasn't like his pa. He'd never taken to books although he could read as well as anyone when he put his mind to it.

"There you are. What are you reading?"

"How are you feeling?" Zach asked without looking up.

"Fine. If I have a problem, I will tell you. What are you reading?"

"A book." Zach turned a page.

"My, is that what they call those?" Lou said in mild exasperation. "Where did you get it and what is it about?"

"My pa gave it to me." Zach held the front of it toward her, keeping his place with his finger. "He said we'd find it useful."

Lou looked but there was no title on the cover. "I still don't know what it's about."

Zach turned it so she could read the title page.

Lou expected it to be one of the James Fenimore Cooper books Nate liked so much but it was *The American Almanac and Repository of Useful Knowledge.* "My word. Why are you reading a thing like that?"

"There's a part in here that has to do with babies. About how to be a good father and mother."

Lou wanted to hug him. He could be such a trial; hardheaded, stubborn, temperamental. Then he'd go and do something sweet, like this. "What does it say?"

"It says here that a newborn should sleep next to the mother for the first eight weeks. It says that the baby sleeps better and puts on more weight than if it sleeps in a crib." Zach looked at her. "I'll rig a cot here in the living room for the other."

"What other?" Lou asked, confused.

"Well, you won't want to do it in bed with the

baby right there, so we can sneak out when it's sleeping and use the cot."

"It?" Lou said, and then realized what he was referring to. "My God. The baby's not even born yet. It won't be born for pretty near eight months. And you're thinking of *that*?"

"One of us has to plan ahead."

Lou went from wanting to hug him to wanting to slug him. "Why you . . . you . . ." She couldn't think of a word fitting enough. ". . . you *male*, you."

Zach lowered his legs and sat up. "What are you getting so hot about? Here I am trying to make things easier for us. I offered to build a cot, didn't I?"

"Easier for *you*," Lou said. In a huff she marched to the front door. "I need some air."

Zach didn't help matters by sighing and saying, "Women sure are prickly when they're pregnant."

Lou balled her fists. If there was anything in this world more aggravating than men, she had yet to meet it. She flung the door wide. Here and there were scattered puddles, but for the most part the ground around their cabin was clear. It sat on a slight elevation, no more than a few inches above the rest of the shore, but that was enough. Rainwater invariably drained toward the lake.

Without paying much attention, Lou stalked out and went a few yards and stopped to take deep breaths.

Something hissed near her leg.

Lou glanced down and couldn't credit her eyes.

Rattlesnakes were on all sides of her.

Winona King was wrapping a pie in a cloth to keep it warm. Her husband was fond of pies. Early in their marriage she had learned of his fondness and practiced until she could bake them exactly as he liked them. Her own people didn't have anything like them, and she had to admit, they were delicious. She carefully placed the pie in the basket and was closing the lid when she snapped her head up and said, "A shot."

Nate had heard it, too. He was at the table, honing his Bowie. He put the whetstone down and went out, leaving the door open for her to follow, as he knew she would.

"Which direction, do you think?" Winona asked. His ears were much better than hers.

Nate pointed to the northeast at a point along the shore. "Somewhere over yonder."

"From Zach's?"

"No. Farther along." Nate rose onto the tips of his toes, but other than his son's cabin the opposite shore was a vague line of rock and earth, and beyond, the green of the trees.

"Rifle or pistol?"

"Pistol."

"Did Evelyn take her rifle?"

"She forgot again. I noticed too late, after she was gone."

"But she had her pistols?"

"I know what you're thinking." Nate went inside, snatched his Hawken from where he had propped it, and came back out. "I'll have a look."

"I'll go with you."

"No need," Nate said. "I won't be long. You can finish getting ready."

"But if it's Evelyn . . ."

"If she was in real trouble, we'd hear more shots or shouts or screams," Nate said. His secret dread was that one day one of his family would be harmed. It didn't help that had hardly a month went by that some danger or other didn't rear its unwanted head.

Winona was torn between going and staying. She gazed across the lake, its surface serene now that the thunderhead had moved on. She looked to the northwest, at the Worths' far-off cabin, and then to the north at her son's, and at the stretch of shore that curled away from their own toward the others— and her breath caught in her throat. "Husband?"

Nate was almost to the corner. He stopped and turned. It took a few seconds for what he was seeing to sink in. Water covered much of the ground, inches of it, to within five or six yards of their front door. At first it appeared as if the water was moving, but it wasn't the water, it was something *in* the water. He took a few steps and the shapes acquired form. "It can't be," he blurted.

"You see them, then?"

Nate nodded. Snakes. Rattlesnakes. Hundreds of the things, swimming, crawling, moving aimlessly about as if they had no sense of where they should go. "God in heaven."

Winona was aghast. She had never seen so many at one time. The whole shore was covered. Washed from somewhere by the rain, she suspected. "You were right about the hunt," she said. "There must have been a den close by. If only we had found it."

Small consolation for Nate. He was thinking of the shot they heard. One shot, and nothing else. "Stay here. Close the door and keep it closed." He ran around the cabin to the corral. A large rattler was coiled almost at his feet. Drawing his Bowie, he hefted it, cocked his arm, and threw. The razor tip

sliced into the serpent's blunt head between its alien
eyes and cleaved the skull nearly in half. The body
whipped wildly back and forth.

Winona came running up. She had gone in for her
own rifle and rushed back out. Bending, she yanked
the Bowie loose and held the hilt toward him. "We
must get to her right away."

"Me," Nate said. "Not we."

"She is my daughter, too." Winona turned to the
gate.

"I'd rather you didn't."

"Give me one good reason."

Nate recited several. "It's dangerous enough for
one person. We can't afford to lose two horses. And
if McNair or Waku and his family show up, someone should be here to warn them about the snakes."

"I am going," Winona insisted.

"I can't watch out for you and me, both."

"Who asked you to? I can take care of myself, as
you well know."

"What about Shakespeare and the Nansusequas?"

"They are not stupid. They will see the snakes
and avoid them just as we will."

Nate knew better, but he asked, "There's nothing I
can say or do, is there, to change your mind?"

"Not a thing. Nothing will keep me from my
daughter. Not the Great Mystery. Not the snakes. Not
you, husband, as much as I love you." Winona gestured. "We are wasting precious time. Our daughter
might need us."

"Saddles?" Nate said.

"More wasted time. We can ride bareback."

Nate slid bridles on his bay and her mare. He led
the pair out and climbed on the bay. Winona swung

onto her mare and together they went around the cabin and promptly drew rein.

"How will we get past all those snakes?" Winona wondered.

Nate had been thinking about that. The rattlers were virtually everywhere except for a narrow strip along the lake—and *in* the lake itself. "Stay behind me." He reined toward the water and rode at a slow walk. Between the cabin and the lake the snakes weren't as thick, but there were enough to make him nervous. The thud of the bay's heavy hooves sent most of them gliding away. A few hissed but didn't stand their ground.

"Look out!" Winona cried.

One of the snakes had coiled and raised its head to strike.

Chapter Sixteen

Evelyn King pulsed with fear. She tried to stand, but her left leg was pinned. The horse lay unmoving and silent save for the rasp of its labored breathing. "Please, no," Evelyn said. She pushed against the sorrel. She pushed harder. She might as well push a mountain.

The rattler kept coming. It was crawling straight for her, its tongue constantly flicking.

Evelyn stabbed her hand for her other flintlock. Terror seized her as she realized it was gone. She glanced about her, but it was nowhere to be seen. Maybe it was under the horse, she thought. She groped for her knife in its sheath on her left hip, but she couldn't pull the blade free. It was wedged tight by her weight and she couldn't rise high enough to work it free. She gave a last frantic tug, and the snake reached her.

Evelyn turned to stone. She expected it to coil and bite. Instead, it crawled up onto her shoulder. She shuddered at the contact and immediately willed herself to stop in case it provoked the snake into striking. The rattler went crawling on past as if she were a rock or a log.

"God," Evelyn breathed, and grinned. She had been lucky, awful lucky. She pushed at the saddle and at the sorrel with the same result as before. Tiring, she sank onto her back and stared at the sky. She needed help. She couldn't extricate herself alone.

Rising onto her elbows, she went to shout—and new fear gushed through her like spears of ice.

More snakes were emerging from the pool and making for the woods. Six, seven, eight of them, six rattlers and a bull snake and another that might be a ribbon snake. They crawled with purpose, their heads slightly raised, forked tongues darting.

Evelyn choked off a cry as the foremost viper crawled over the sorrel's neck and onto her chest. It was so close to her face, she could have stuck out her own tongue and licked it. Rigid with fright, she didn't breathe. She saw the vertical slits in its eyes, she saw every scale. The feel of it brushing across her body was almost more than she could bear. No sooner was it off her when another smaller rattler took its place. This one, too, went over her without a sideways look. A third rattler slithered over the sorrel and onto her. It was thicker than the others, the skin pattern not the same. The head came even with her chin—and the rattler stopped and swung its head toward her.

Evelyn resisted an impulse to scream and throw it off. She started to swallow and caught herself. The snake's tongue was an inch from her throat. She prayed it would keep going but it just lay there, staring. Its mouth opened and she braced for the pain of its fangs, but all it did was hiss and continue on. She closed her eyes tight and fought back tears. When she opened them, the snake was off her.

Evelyn didn't know how much of this she could stand. The other snakes had gone wide of her, but there were bound to be more. She pushed at the sorrel with all the strength in her, but it wasn't enough. Exhausted, she sank onto her back and closed her eyes again. She couldn't imagine where all the snakes had come from. She didn't really care. She wanted away from there, to be with Dega, to have him hold her in his arms. She liked being in his arms more than she had ever liked anything. It felt so good, so comforting. She wondered if she would ever see him again. The thought of not seeing him brought an ache to her chest, a hurt so powerful it was as if her heart were being crushed.

Something was on her arm.

Evelyn opened her eyes and wished she hadn't. A veritable legion of snakes were streaming out of the pool and nearby puddles and moving in a body toward the drier sanctuary of the forest floor, so many of them that in places they formed a living carpet of moving scales. She barely had time to brace herself when four of them crawled onto her, moving across her chest, the nearest brushing her chin as it went by.

Tears filled Evelyn's eyes, but she refused to cry. Not with more snakes wriggling onto her. She couldn't look. Again she shut her eyes and felt a serpentine form glide over her neck. Another went over the top of her head. All it would take was for her to sneeze and she was as good as bitten.

Evelyn thought of her father and mother. In the past she had always counted on them to get her out of tight scrapes. Not this time. They were too far away. Even if they heard the shot, they might figure it was someone shooting game and not realize she was in trouble.

"I want to live," Evelyn said softly, and meant every syllable. She nearly gave a start when a snake brushed her throat.

A rattler crawled onto her face.

It was the hardest thing Evelyn ever had to do; to lie there and not twitch a muscle as the rattler slithered across her mouth and cheek and forehead. The scrape of every scale was magnified tenfold. She was scared down to her marrow but dared not react.

Suddenly the snake was off her, but it was only a temporary reprieve. More were crawling toward her. A lot more.

God, Evelyn thought. She couldn't take much more of this. It would drive her insane.

Chickory Worth's eyes nearly bugged out of his head. They weren't just any old snakes crawling around his feet. They were *rattlesnakes*. Chickory yelped and kicked and jumped backward. A couple of bounds and he would be inside. But as he sprang a sharp pain shot up his leg and when he landed he felt another snake under him and looked down just as it sank its fangs into his right foot. Chickory screeched, as much in terror as from the hurt, and threw himself at the doorway. He stumbled through, slammed the door behind him, and sprawled onto his hands and knees.

"What in the world?" Emala exclaimed, sitting up.

"Snakes!" Chickory gasped. "Rattlers! I've been bitten!" He sat and extended his legs.

Emala was speechless with shock for a few moments. Letting out a shriek of dismay, she smacked Samuel's shoulder, bawling, "Get up! Get up! Our boy's done been snakebit!" Despite her bulk she was the first to reach Chickory and kneel beside him. "Where?" she bleated. "Where were you bit?"

Chickory pointed. The bite marks were plain to see; two red dots on his right foot and two more on his left calf. "Twice," he said. "They're all over out there."

Randa ran to the door. Opening it, she looked out and exclaimed, "Oh my God! He's right! They're everywhere."

"Close the door," Samuel commanded. He squatted beside his wife, leaned over his son, and drew his knife.

"What are you fixin' to do?" Emala asked in wide-eyed horror.

"Suck the poison out like they do with cottonmouths." Samuel cut an X above the bite marks on Chickory's calf and pressed his mouth to the incision. Blood welled, and he sucked a mouthful and spat it out.

"What if you get poison in you?" Emala asked. "I've heard tell of that happenin'."

"Has to be done," Samuel said, and sucked another mouthful.

Emala clasped her hands to her bosom and raised her eyes to the roof. "Hear me, Lord. Spare my son. I pray you'll spare my husband, too. Save them from that awful venom. Don't take them away from me now, when we are startin' our new home."

"Hush, will you?" Samuel said, and sucked a third mouthful.

Appalled by his lack of courtesy, Emala said, "Don't be interrupin' me when I'm talkin' to the Lord. Do you want him mad at us?"

Randa came over and placed her hand on her brother's arm. "How do you feel?"

"How do you think I feel?" Chickory retorted. "I've just been bit by two rattlers. I'm dyin'."

Louisa King stayed calm. Turning her head, she called out, "Zach, I need you."

Zach put down the book and walked to the doorway. He thought maybe she wanted to go riding and needed him to saddle her horse. She could do it herself except he insisted on doing it for her. He was smiling to show he wasn't bothered by their little tiff. "What do you—" he began, and stopped, his breath catching in his throat at the sight he beheld: snakes, snakes and more snakes. From what he could see, most were rattlers. Several were near Lou's feet. Instantly he drew his tomahawk and his Bowie.

"Don't move. I'm coming for you."

Lou didn't argue. A large rattler was circling her as if it couldn't decide whether she was something it should bite. She recalled that not all bites were fatal, but even so, all that venom in her body wouldn't be good for the baby in her womb. "God, no," she said.

Zach counted six snakes near enough to her that they might strike if she moved. Clearing the threshold in a bound, he was among them. He arced the tomahawk at a thick neck. He sheared the Bowie at another. Spinning, he cleaved a viper just as it was coiling, slashed a fourth as the snake turned toward him. The largest and the nearest to her raised its ugly head and he severed the head from the body with a sideways swipe. The last turned to flee and he chopped it into three pieces with three swift cuts. Then he had Lou in his arms and was flying into the cabin and kicking the door shut behind them.

Lou clung to him. She had been terrified that he would be bitten. He was quick, so very, very quick, but there had been so many rattlers, she'd worried that even his speed might not have been enough. "Thank you," she breathed into his neck.

"I have some uses," Zach said.

"Never said you didn't." Lou kissed him. "You can put me down. I'm all right."

Zach placed her in a chair and went to the window. "There must be hundreds. Thousands, even."

Lou was thinking of something else. "Do you remember we heard a horse go by a while ago?"

Zach nodded.

"And then there was that shot. Do you think . . ." Lou didn't finish. The implication was obvious.

Zach turned. He mentally kicked himself for not going out and seeing who had ridden by; he had been lying in bed with Lou. "I doubt it was any of the Worths. They had no reason to be out and about so soon after the storm."

"Your mother or your father?"

"Ma or Pa would have stopped." Zach had a troubling thought. "Whoever it was, they were headed east toward Waku's lodge."

They looked at each other and both of them said at the same time, "Evelyn."

Zach was still holding his tomahawk and Bowie. He went to the door and paused with a finger on the latch. "Stay inside, you hear me? I won't brook an argument. If you won't do it for me or you won't do it for yourself, do it for the baby."

Lou nodded. "Don't worry." She stood and came over. "I wish you didn't have to."

"She's my sister."

"You're going without your rifle?" Lou nodded at the Hawken in the corner.

Zach hefted his edged weapons. "These are better. I can kill more, faster." He worked the latch.

"Be careful, darn you," Lou said anxiously, and kissed him hard on the mouth. "Our baby needs a pa."

"I don't aim to die." Zach smiled and slipped out and shut the door behind him.

Lou leaned her forehead against it and closed her eyes in dread. The thing was, there was no guarantee he wouldn't.

Nate jerked his Hawken to his shoulder and fired. The heavy ball hit smack in the center of the rattlesnake's head and the head exploded. The path to the lake was momentarily clear. He reloaded as he rode. He goaded the bay into the water, reined parallel with the shore, and brought it to a gallop. Winona was right behind him.

Nate was astounded at the number of snakes he saw and relieved that they didn't come near the lake. Rattlers could swim, but it was his understanding they only did so when pressed or after prey. Most of the time they fought shy of water. A lot of the snakes, he noticed, were crawling toward the forest to get out of the wet and the chill.

Moments like this, Nate almost regretted living in the wilderness. There was always something, always some new threat to deal with. He yearned for a spell of peace and quiet, a long spell where none of his family or his friends were in peril.

That was the crucial difference between the wilderness and civilization. People who lived in cities and towns and on farms back East could go their entire lives without anything to fear save old age. Oh, a wagon might roll over or a horse go down or they might come down with a disease, but for the most part their lives were peaceful.

The wilderness was anything *but* peaceful. It was a savage realm of fang and claw where the only true peace was the peace of the grave. Yet God help him,

Nate loved it. Not the savagery, but the freedom that came from living without laws and rules. The only restraints were those he imposed on himself.

It was freedom in its purest sense, and more precious to him than the security of civilized society.

A long time ago, when the children were small, Nate had asked Winona if she would rather live east of the Mississippi where there were fewer dangers. She had stopped sewing and looked at him with that special look of hers and said that danger had always been part of her existence. She couldn't let fear of it rule her. Life was for living, not hiding.

"Husband! Look!"

Nate came out of his reverie. They were on the north side of the lake. Ahead was his son's cabin. Lou was at the window, waving her arms.

"We should stop!" Winona called.

Reluctantly, Nate slowed. He would only take a minute and be on his way. Whoever had fired that shot might need help. Any delay could prove fatal.

Chapter Seventeen

Snakes were all over her.

Evelyn held herself still and clenched her fists and bit her lower lip so hard she drew a drop of blood, all in an effort to keep from screaming and flailing. Serpents were on her arms, her chest, her head. She never knew when one might sense she was a threat and attack.

The sorrel stopped breathing. A last gasp, its tongue lolled from its mouth, and it was gone.

Evelyn would have wept if she wasn't so afraid. Here she had always thought of herself as somewhat brave. She'd faced buffalo and bears and an alligator once and survived people trying to kill her, and none of that filled her with the fear and loathing *this* did. Having snake after snake crawl over her, having their bodies brush her clothes and rub her skin—she could barely stand it.

Their number became fewer and fewer until at long last she had none on her. She hoped that was the end of them, that they had all gone into the woods, but she was mistaken.

Out of the pool came five more, some of the biggest yet, crawling slowly but inexorably toward her and the poor sorrel.

"Please, no," Evelyn pleaded, and squeezed her eyes tight shut. Maybe if she didn't watch them it wouldn't affect her as much. She heard them, though, heard the scrape of scales on cloth and a hiss. One crawled onto her arm. Her natural reaction was to jerk her arm away, but she commanded herself not to move. The snake wriggled onto her chest, and stopped.

Evelyn almost sobbed. She waited for it to move on and when it didn't, she cracked her eyelids. The thing was huge, as thick around as her pa's arm. Its head was a few inches from her face and it was flicking its tongue as if testing the air. *Keep going,* she mentally begged. *Please keep going.*

The rattler didn't move. It looked around and then lay back down with its lower jaw on her shoulder.

Dear God, Evelyn thought. It was resting on her. It must like how warm her body was after the cold of the water. She suppressed an impulse to shudder. She mustn't so much as twitch. But how long could she stay still? Evelyn asked herself. Her nerves were raw. She was frayed to where she might lose control. *Please,* she prayed, *make it go away.*

The rattler started to coil. She tensed, expecting it to attack, but no, it coiled in on itself and lay on her chest with its head on top of its coils. It wasn't going anywhere. It might stay on her for the rest of the day, for all she knew.

Evelyn couldn't take it. She just couldn't. She knew that if she screamed or she moved it would make the snake mad, but her need to get it off overwhelmed her reason. Torn from her innermost being, ripped from her against her will, a keening shriek burst from her lips. Simultaneously, she swatted at the snake with all her might and sent it tumbling onto the ground. For a span of heartbeats she felt sheer elation. It was off her! She was safe!

A hiss shattered the illusion.

Evelyn twisted her head.

The rattler had coiled and its tail was buzzing like a hundred angry hornets. Its baleful eyes fixed on her and it poised to strike.

Zach King stood at the rear corner of his cabin, his Bowie in his left hand, his tomahawk in his right. Before him were puddles and pools teeming with snakes. Many of the reptiles were making for the trees. If he waited a while, the shore would be clear, but he couldn't shake a persistent feeling that his sister was in trouble. He must get to her quickly.

Taking a deep breath, Zach bounded forward. He vaulted a viper, skirted another. A thick one reared in his path and he separated its head from its body. To the right was a clear space. A few steps, and he jumped over several rattlers entwined together. He tried not to think of how many there were. He tried not to dwell on the consequences of being bitten. He thought only of Evelyn, and of not letting anything stop him from reaching her.

The next stretch was clear of water and almost clear of rattlers. He ran faster. Well to the east a mound caught his eye, a mound where none had been before. He couldn't quite make out what it was and he couldn't keep staring at it with snakes to watch out for.

A lot of small pools and puddles appeared, pools and puddles writhing with serpents.

Zach stopped. It would be easier to go around. He turned toward the lake and glanced at the strange mound again—and his pulse quickened. He had realized what it was; a horse, on its side. And when he squinted he could make out a part of a saddle.

"Evelyn," Zach said, and flew toward it. He didn't care that there were rattlesnakes in his path. He didn't see his sister and that meant she must be down, too, and nothing, absolutely nothing, was going to stop him from reaching her. He slashed a rattler, sidestepped, cut another, took several long bounds and cleared a moving rug of scaly death. He landed, swung, rent a reptilian head, spun, chopped another in half and was in motion even as the blow landed.

He didn't dare stop, didn't dare relax, didn't dare relent. He must stay on the move so he was harder to bite. Speed and reflexes, they were the key. He mustn't think. He mustn't worry about Evelyn. He hacked. He cut. Always in motion, always slicing. There were so many snakes. So very many. For every serpent he slew there were ten more.

A big one with green markings lashed at his foot. He jumped and struck as he alighted, his tomahawk splitting its skull as neatly as a butcher knife split red meat. Then he was on the move again, running, jumping, dodging, evading. He was closer to the horse, but he couldn't look at it. Not yet. Not until he was there.

More rattlers bared his way. Those heading for the forest paid no attention to him unless he came near them and then most hissed and a few coiled, but they didn't attack. He cleared a knot of ten or more and in front of him were a pair of thick ones, one on his right and the other on his left, big and coiled and their tails buzzing chorus. Both struck at his legs and Zach leaped straight up as high as he could leap. The two snakes flashed under his moccasins. He came down on top of them, slamming his right foot on the neck of the one and his left foot onto the head of the other. Instantly he speared the Bowie in and drove the tomahawk down. Then he was off and running, jumping, spinning.

I'm coming, Evelyn, he thought. *I'm coming for you.*

Chickory Worth couldn't understand it. He had been biten twice. The bites hurt like the dickens. But he was still breathing. Even more amazing, except for where he'd been bitten, he didn't feel anything. He wasn't numb or tingly or itchy or in much pain.

Emala had her hands clasped to her bosom and was rocking on her knees and praying at the top of her lungs. Tears trickled down her cheeks. "Hear me, Lord. I beg you. Spare him. He's my only boy. Don't let him die by no serpents. Serpents are Satan's brood and the Bible says that those who have faith are proof against their poison."

"Please, Ma," Chickory said.

Emala raised her hands over her head. "I pray my faith is true. I pray you will heal him. I pray for your blessin' in this as I pray for your blessin' in all there is. Please, Lord, help us."

Samuel had stopped sucking and was sitting with his hands propped behind him. Spittle glistened on his lower lip and chin. "I don't know as I got it all out, but I tried my best, Son."

"I know you did, Pa."

Randa hunkered and examined Chickory's leg. "There's no swellin' yet. I think I heard they swell sometimes."

"How do you feel?" Samuel asked.

"Except for where they bit, I feel fine. I don't feel nothin'."

"Nothin'?"

"Not a thing, Pa. It could be you got all the poison out. It could be you saved my life."

"Or it could be there wasn't any poison to begin with," Samuel said. "I didn't taste any. But then, I ain't exactly sure what snake poison tastes like."

"I was bit," Chickory said.

"Sure you were. But Nate King told me that rattlers don't always . . ." Samuel stopped. "What was the word he used? Oh. Yes. Rattlers don't always inject their poison. Sometimes they just bite and that's all."

"Please hear me, God!" Emala wailed. "The Lord is my shepherd, I shall not want. Unto thee, oh Lord, do I lift up my soul. I will praise thee, oh Lord, with all my heart. Have mercy upon me, oh Lord. Have mercy upon my son."

"Emala," Samuel said.

"Hearken unto the voice of my cry, my King and my God, for unto thee will I pray. My voice shalt thou hear in the mornin', oh Lord."

"Emala?"

"Yea, though I walk through the valley of the shadow of death, I will fear no evil. For thou art with me. Thy rod and thy staff they comfort me. Thou preparest a table—"

Samuel gripped her arm. "Stop your caterwaulin' and listen to me, woman."

Emala opened her eyes and recoiled as if he had slapped her. "Did you just call my prayin' *caterwaulin'*?"

"He's all right."

"Here I am, tryin' the best I know how to persuade the Lord to help us, and you go and blaspheme." Emala shrugged off his hand. "You're beginnin' to worry me, Samuel Worth. You truly are. Don't you give a fig about your eternal soul?"

"Chickory is all right."

"The Lord don't like blasphemin'. It says so right in the Bible. He'll forgive a heap of things but not that. You'd best get on your knees and beg him to forgive you or—" Emala blinked. "What did you say?"

"Our son is fine."

"He is?" Emala turned to Chickory, new tears shimmering in her eyes. "Is that true? The poison isn't makin' you turn all blue and choke on your tongue?"

"The bites sting some, is all," Chickory answered. "But I'm breathin' fine."

"Land sakes." Emala grasped Samuel's arm and nearly jerked him off balance. "Do you know what this is?"

"We were lucky," Samuel said.

Emala vigorously shook her head. "None are so blind as those that won't see. Luck had nothin' to do with it." She reverently put her hand on Chickory's calf and said in awe, "This was a miracle."

"What?" Samuel said.

"You heard me. A miracle. Just like in the Bible when Jesus healed the sick and Moses parted the Red Sea." Emala ran her fingers over the bites as if caressing them. "Our very own miracle right here in our family. That I should live to see somethin' so wondrous."

"The snakes only bit him, is all," Samuel explained.

"Of course they bit him. I can see the holes."

"No. I mean they bit him, but they didn't get their poison into him," Samuel said. "Haven't you been payin' attention? That's why he's not dyin'."

"He's not dyin' because the Lord heard my prayer." Emala raised her arms on high. "We must give thanks. When we go to church we—" She stopped and her eyes widened. "Glory be. I just realized. We don't have a church to go to."

"Ministers don't come to the Rockies," Samuel said. "I doubt there will be a church hereabouts for a hundred years or better."

"We can't have that," Emala said. "We need a house of worship. I bet if we had one, the Kings and the McNairs would come and maybe those Nansusequas if we asked them real nice, even if they are heathens."

"But we don't have one, so why bring it up?"

"We don't have one now, but we will." Emala beamed and nodded. "We're going to build one."

"What?" Samuel said.

"What?" Randa echoed.

"You heard me," Emala declared.

Chickory groaned and put his hand on his leg as if the pain had made him do it.

"Listen to yourself, woman," Samuel scoffed. "You can't just build your own church."

"It wouldn't be just for me," Emala said. "It'd be for everyone. Since there's not a lot of us, it wouldn't need to be big. We could even add a room to our cabin and have it be the church."

"Are you sure you weren't the one snakebit?"

Emala bristled like a kicked porcupine. "Samuel Worth, you don't fool me. You don't want to have to go to church every Sunday. You were a shirker back on the plantation and you are a shirker still."

"You better ask Mr. King what he thinks."

"I don't need to ask Mr. King. I have my answer right here." Emala patted Chickory's leg. "The Lord himself has given us a sign."

"The snake bite?"

"The miracle. It's the Lord's way of showing us

we're all under his care and we shouldn't forget him just because we're in the middle of nowhere without a church."

Samuel stared.

"Why are you lookin' at me like that? I'm right and you know it. King Valley needs a house of worship. Maybe we can have a bell hauled in and every Sunday morning Chickory can ring it to call everyone together." Emala couldn't wait. "It'll be marvelous. We'll have pews and a pulpit and we'll even get our hands on hymn books."

"What about a minister?" Samuel brought up. "Where do you expect to find one out here in the middle of nowhere, as you called it."

"That's easy," Emala said. "One of us will have to take charge of the services, and there's only one person in this whole valley who's qualified."

"Mr. McNair?" Randa said.

"No, silly." Emala laughed with delight. "Me."

Chickory gripped his leg and groaned louder.

Evelyn King stared death in its reptilian face. The rattlesnake had reared to strike. She'd heard tell that rattlers didn't open their mouths until the moment they struck, but this one did, baring its lethal fangs. A drop of venom fell from each one. She went to fling up her arm when there was a flash of light and the viper's head plopped to the ground. There was another flash and another and pieces of the snake joined the head. A buckskin-clad figure blotted out the sun and a hand gently touched her cheek.

"I'm here, little sister," Zach said.

Evelyn gripped his hand and held it to her cheek and closed her eyes and held back tears.

"There are more coming."

Evelyn let go and Zach stepped over her and put himself between her and the snakes. In one hand was his gore-spattered tomahawk, in the other his gore-spattered Bowie. Both weapons became blurs. She lost count of how many he killed, marveling the whole while at how quick he was, and how unerring his aim.

Evelyn knew that her brother was widely feared by whites and red men alike, and seeing him now, as he hacked and split and cut every rattlesnake that came near her, it wasn't hard to see why. She would never say it to his face, but Zach was a natural-born killer. For long minutes he proved her right. Then, at last, he straightened and wearily turned.

"That was the last of them."

Evelyn burst into tears. Tears of relief and joy combined. She cried quietly until she was drained and couldn't shed another drop. Sniffling, she dabbed at her nose with her sleeve. "I must look a sight."

Zach chuckled. "You're sort of cute with snot all over your face."

Despite herself, Evelyn laughed.

Zach set down the tomahawk and Bowie and pushed at the saddle. "When I get this high enough, do you think you can pull your leg out?"

"I'll try," Evelyn said. "But I can't feel anything. For all I know, it's broken."

"Let's try." Zach squatted and slid his arms as far under the sorrel as he could and grit his teeth and strained. His face grew red and his shoulders and neck bulged.

Evelyn braced herself on her elbows. The pressure eased slightly and she pulled. Her leg slid an inch or so, and no farther. She tried harder and finally shook her head and said, "It's not working."

"Damn." Zach eased off and draped his forearms over his knees. "I need help."

At that juncture hooves pounded and a big bay came to a halt and a giant form vaulted down.

"Pa!" Evelyn squealed.

Nate King was a study in concern. He looked from his daughter to his son and back again. "Are both of you all right?" He stared at Evelyn. "You?"

"We're fine, Pa. I can't get loose, though."

"You will now." Nate squatted and said to Zach, "When I lift, you pull her out."

"You don't want me to help you?"

"No need, Son."

Evelyn had long known her father was immensely strong, but even she was amazed when he slid his hands under the horse as Zach had done and his shoulders and neck swelled and the weight came off her. Zach took hold under her arms and eased her out from under and when she was clear he said, "She's out, Pa. You did it."

Nate examined her leg. "It doesn't appear to be broken. Can you move it any?"

"Give me a minute." Evelyn was tingling from her hips to her toes. From the flow of blood being restored, she reckoned. It almost tickled. She wriggled her toes. "The feeling is coming back."

Zach glanced at the forest. "Where did all those snakes come from? I never imagined there were so many."

"A den somewhere," Nate said. "We may never know exactly where. The rain brought them out, I suspect."

"Will they go back to it or find another?"

"I don't know." Nate indicated his bay. "I want you to ride to Waku's and then to Shakespeare's and tell them to come as fast as they can to your cabin. Your mother is there with Lou. We're going to have another snake hunt and kill as many as we can before they find cover."

Zach nodded and collected his tomahawk and Bowie. A lithe swing, and he was up and away.

"Why not let them be?" Evelyn asked. "They never did anything like this before. It was the rain that brought them out. You said so yourself."

"You can say that after what you've just been through?"

"It wasn't their fault, Pa. They were just doing what snakes do."

"They were being true to their nature, yes," Nate said. "So is a hungry griz when it charges you, but you would have me shoot the griz, I bet."

"That's different."

"The more rattlers there are, the higher the chance that someday you'll go out to the chicken coop or around to the corral and almost step on one and get bit." Nate shook his head. "I won't have that. I won't let the threat exist. Do you understand?"

"I suppose." Evelyn let herself sink down onto her back. Her ordeal had exhausted her. Suddenly arms were under her, lifting her off the ground. In surprise she blurted, "What are you doing?"

"Taking you to Zach's so your mother and Lou can tend you." Nate strode west, his Hawken in his left hand.

"You don't need to carry me," Evelyn protested. "Give me a few minutes and I'll be able to walk."

"You're soaked clean through and your clothes are a mess and you have snake blood all over you," Nate said. "You need a hot bath and a cup of your mother's healing tea." He looked down at her and grinned. "Besides, Dega will be here soon. Do you really want him to see you looking like this?"

Evelyn hadn't thought of that. "Walk faster," she said. It felt good being in her father's strong arms. He hadn't picked her up in years, not since she went from being a girl to a young woman. She placed her cheek on his chest and looped her arms around his neck. "Thanks, Pa."

"For what?"

"For you and Ma always being there for me."

"Zach, too. Don't forget your brother."

Evelyn saw him again in her mind's eye, the Grim Reaper of rattlers, laying waste right and left to save her from harm. "I love him, too. Don't ever tell him that, though." She gazed out over the lake, bright now in the reborn sun. "You know something? I'm happy here."

"I hope so. It's your home."

"It is, isn't it?" Evelyn snuggled against him. She was feeling sleepy. "Remember when I'd had enough of life in the wild and wanted to go off and live in a city?"

"I remember it well."

"I've changed my mind. Here is as good as anywhere. I think I'll stay for as long as you'll have me."

"That would be forever," Nate said, and pecked her on the forehead.

Evelyn closed her eyes. She was close to drifting off. "There's something I've been meaning to tell you. You and Ma, both. I guess now is as good a time as any."

"About Dega?" Nate said.

Evelyn jerked her head up. "You know about him and me?"

"We've known for some time."

"And you don't mind? You didn't say anything. You didn't try to stop me from seeing him."

"Why would we? Your mother wasn't much older than you when I courted her."

Evelyn smiled and kissed him on the cheek and hugged him. "Thanks, Pa. Thanks for caring so much and being so understanding and all."

"It's what fathers do," Nate King said.

Author's Note

Several of the entries in Nate King's journal are regarded by some as tall tales. His account of the "hairy creatures," for instance, related in an earlier book, and again, his experiences with the NunumBi.

The author brings this up because there are a few who think that Nate's account of the "snake invasion," as a herpetologist called it, is another of those tall tales.

The author would note, however, that dens have been found with hundreds of snakes. In one documented instance (see below) over *20,000* were filmed.

So the snake invasion is not as far-fetched as some would have us believe.

(To see the 20,000 for yourself, go to You Tube and search the term: 20,000 snakes in a Narcisse snake pit.)

INTERACT WITH DORCHESTER ONLINE!

Want to learn more about your favorite books and authors?
Want to talk with other readers that like to read the same books as you?
Want to see up-to-the-minute Dorchester news?

VISIT DORCHESTER AT:

DorchesterPub.com
Twitter.com/DorchesterPub
Facebook.com (Search Pages)

DISCUSS DORCHESTER'S NOVELS AT:

Dorchester Forums at DorchesterPub.com
GoodReads.com
LibraryThing.com
Myspace.com/books
Shelfari.com
WeRead.com

Bill Pronzini & Marcia Muller

The dark clouds are gathering, and it's promising to be a doozy of a storm at the River Bend stage station ... where the owners are anxiously awaiting the return of their missing daughter. Where a young cowboy hopes to find safety from the rancher whose wife he's run away with. Where a Pinkerton agent has tracked the quarry he's been chasing for years. Thunder won't be the only thing exploding along ...

CRUCIFIXION RIVER

Bill Pronzini and Marcia Muller are a husband-wife writing team with numerous individual honors, including the Lifetime Achievement Award from the Private Eye Writers of America, the Grand Master Award from Mystery Writers of America, and the American Mystery Award. In addition to the Spur Award–winning title novella, this volume also contains stories featuring Bill Pronzini's famous "Nameless Detective" and Marcia Muller's highly popular Sharon McCone investigator.

ISBN 13: 978-0-8439-6341-0

✂ ☐ **YES!**

Sign me up for the Leisure Western Book Club and send my FREE BOOKS! If I choose to stay in the club, I will pay only $14.00* each month, a savings of $9.96!

NAME: _____

ADDRESS: _____

TELEPHONE: _____

EMAIL: _____

☐ I want to pay by credit card.

☐ **VISA**   ☐ MasterCard   ☐ DISCOVER

ACCOUNT #: _____

EXPIRATION DATE: _____

SIGNATURE: _____

Mail this page along with $2.00 shipping and handling to:
Leisure Western Book Club
PO Box 6640
Wayne, PA 19087
Or fax (must include credit card information) to:
610-995-9274
You can also sign up online at www.dorchesterpub.com.
*Plus $2.00 for shipping. Offer open to residents of the U.S. and Canada only.
Canadian residents please call 1-800-481-9191 for pricing information.
If under 18, a parent or guardian must sign. Terms, prices and conditions subject to change. Subscription subject to acceptance. Dorchester Publishing reserves the right to reject any order or cancel any subscription.